ZANE PRESENTS

OUR FIRST LOVE

BROTHERS SHARING ONE LOVE...

A NOVEL

D0124957

ANTHONY LAMARR

SBI

STREBOR BOOKS

NEW YORK LONDON TORONTO SYDNEY

Strebor Books
P.O. Box 6505
Largo, MD 20792
http://www.streborbooks.com

ISBN 978-1-59309-542-0
ISBN 978-1-4767-4727-9 (ebook)

First Strebor Books trade paperback edition December 2013

Cover design: www.mariondesigns.com
Cover photograph: © Keith Saunders/Marion Designs

10 9 8 7 6 5 4 3 2 1

Manufactured in the United States of America

For information regarding special discounts for bulk purchases,
please contact Simon & Schuster Special Sales at 1-866-506-1949
or business@simonandschuster.com

The Simon & Schuster Speakers Bureau can bring authors to your live event.
For more information or to book an event, contact the Simon & Schuster Speakers
Bureau at 1-866-248-3049 or visit our website at www.simonspeakers.com.

The longest, most enduring relationships of my life have been with my brothers. They were my first loves.

For My First Loves
My Brothers
Ken, Tony & Lester
Always

THE CICADA

Every thirteen years in the Southern states, the adult periodical cicada, a subterranean insect, emerges for the first time since taking residency underground, spreads its large amber wings, and begins its frenzied search for a mate. Soon after mating, the cicada falls to the earth and dies. Upon hatching, the orphaned nymphs conceived during these spirited months burrow into the ground and remain there—living a veiled existence—until their own insatiable hunger for love drives them to the surface. To the skies. Into eternity. Thirteen years later.

PROLOGUE

The truth was, I would have loved her anyway. Even if I had known what I know today—that she would abscise us and send our world spiraling out of orbit—I would have still walked that contorted line, fought in vain to hold on to her, and lived again.

Loving her did more than change our lives. Her love changed everything. Time was no longer merely an obdurate reminder of our existence. Minutes. Hours. Days. Weeks. Months. Time didn't exist. So, the tragedy of loving her was not all the conversions she brought to our lives. The real heartbreak was that even in the absence of time, there was an ending: a denouement that left us with no tomorrows.

I didn't know who I had become, but I was certainly not the man I was before I met her. On the rare occasion when I was able to summon enough courage to look in the mirror, I barely recognized the anguished reflection staring back. His pain felt like mine. And his tears stung the same. So, he and I must have been...me.

The sun leered like a Peeping Tom through my window this morning. My T-shirt and boxers were saturated with the anesthetizing sweat of a hangover brought on by way too many cocktails of darkness and excavated memories. And I was tired...so tired that it hurt to simply be. But my heart—against my will—beat the same. Seventy-three. Seventy-four. Seventy-five beats per minute. Meaning, I was still here. Still here. Still here.

SUMMER

CHAPTER 1 ✧ NIGEL

A week ago today, the front page of the *Capitol Sentinel* blared, *Aman Tops Polls in Governor's Race*. And, I was predicting the next day's front page would howl, *Aman Commits Suicide*, while the sidebar wailed, *Reporter Tried to Stop Shooting*.

My left eye twitched as I stood in the doorway staring at the dispirited body slumped over in a wicker chair facing the window. The corpse was dressed in Barney's trademark navy blue suit, white shirt, and garish red tie, but the forty-two-year-old dynamo that inspired swarms of complacent adults into social and political activism was not there. I didn't expect Barney to be home when I rushed inside his voguish chateau on a cul-de-sac in Northwood Plantation. Barney was taking off as soon as the phone went dead.

I wasn't at my desk when Barney called; my editor, Lillian Faulk, answered the phone. I was sitting in the lounge watching *Oprah* and eating a late lunch when Lillian summoned me over the intercom. "Nigel. Nine-one-one at your desk. Now!" I sensed the panic in her voice.

Lillian was frantic, waving the phone when I sprinted into the newsroom. She covered the mouthpiece and yelled, "Hurry, Nigel! Hurry!"

"Is it Caleb? Is something wrong?"

"No! No," she quickly answered. "It's Barney Aman. He's really upset."

Bobby Leno, the newspaper's managing editor, and Russell Lane, city editor, stood behind Lillian. It was Russell's idea for Bobby to temporarily pull me away from features to write personality profiles of Florida's gubernatorial candidates. I wasn't overly thrilled about the assignment, but as usual, I agreed without complaining.

Lillian shoved the phone at me and whispered, "Something's wrong. I'm talking big-time wrong!"

I grabbed the receiver.

"Barney?"

He didn't respond, but somehow I could hear him contemplating what to say.

"Barney, this is Nigel. Is something...?"

"The masquerade is over," Barney blurted out. Like a waxing tidal wave, he divulged, "There's nowhere for me to hide anymore, Nigel."

"What's happened?"

"It won't end with you, Nigel," he cried. "You can't stop it."

I leaned closer to my desk and tried to whisper. "Listen, Barney. I haven't told anyone so you're okay for now."

"What haven't you told?" Russell turned my chair around until I was facing him. "Answer me! What didn't you tell?"

Barney's two lives collided yesterday, but I couldn't tell Russell or Bobby or even Lillian about the manila envelope that had landed liked a missile on my desk. They'd never understand why I didn't say anything about the document inside the envelope or why I'd stopped by Barney's house after work and given him the envelope and its contents. Bobby would've fired me on the spot if he knew that I'd turned my back on the biggest political news story to hit Florida's capital city since Governor Charlie Crist announced his candidacy for the United States Senate instead of seeking another term as Governor.

After the 2008 presidential election, the public called for change, and Barney answered the call. The son of a former congressman,

Barney made his first foray into the world of politics. Even though he was a newcomer, the last-minute announcement of his bid for Governor was met with enthusiasm and hype. Four weeks later, several statewide polls indicated the former star collegiate linebacker was his party's top candidate and, of the seven party candidates, the only one strong enough to win the gubernatorial race. It was apparent, even after his unremarkable two-year stint in the National Football League, that Barney had the makings of a leader. Charisma, good looks, and candor were inherent attributes that made Barney a beacon for voter adoration, media attention, and territorial backlash.

A framed photo of Barney and his parents was on the corpse's lap. Part of Mrs. Aman's face and some of the gold rose petals adorning the frame were covered in her son's blood. The gun, a black pistol with a silver handle, was on the floor beside his feet. Barney's shoes? Barney wasn't wearing any shoes. Where were his shoes? A man like Barney would not go to his death half-dressed. Then, I remembered Barney had two lives, and maybe the Barney I didn't know was more relaxed and blasé.

Lillian tried not to look at the corpse as she stealthily canvassed the room, but I couldn't help staring at it and answering the questions Caleb would ask when I replayed our day for him.

Where did the bullet enter? Below the right eye.

Did it exit? Yes.

Was there a note? A note. A note?

Lillian was already two steps ahead of me. She stood by the desk looking down at Barney's handwritten suicide note. I read the expression on her face. The note left her with more questions than answers.

"We need both of you to leave." A sheriff's deputy walked in Barney's library. "This is a crime scene."

The deputy ushered us out the house and into *Sentinel* photographer Marc Dunwoody's front-page snapshot.

"Thank you, Nigel, for understanding," Lillian blurted out as soon as we got in the car. "That's all he wrote." Lillian backed out of the driveway. "So, are you ready to fill me in?"

Russell and Bobby felt that I had become part of the story, so I was no longer the reporter. Now, Lillian was the reporter, and I was expected to be her exclusive informant.

"You know more than you're saying," Lillian said as she effortlessly steered the car into the bumper-to-bumper traffic on Thomasville Road. "Especially, since you haven't said a word."

I couldn't get the image of Barney's bare feet out of my head. He was always impeccably dressed, even when he appeared at casual events like last week's Juneteenth festivities at Tom Brown Park. Barney and a slew of parading candidates and aloof dignitaries were there to welcome the overflowing crowd to the city's annual freedom celebration. It was ninety-eight degrees by noon, so everyone dressed in shorts, T-shirts and sundresses. Barney was the exception. Wearing stiff khakis and a long-sleeved white oxford, he was...

"What did you understand?" Lillian yelled to get my attention.

"Sorry, Lil. What did you say?"

"'*Thank you, Nigel, for understanding.*' That's all Barney wrote in his suicide note. And I'm guessing that means you knew what he was hiding. So, talk to me."

"I can't..."

"Why not?" Lillian's sympathetic repose was a camouflage. "I'm listening."

Vehicles in the northbound lanes slowed down and pulled off

the road as flashing lights and a shrieking siren neared. The ambulance was less than a mile from Barney's house but, regrettably, a spent hour too late to be of any help.

"Did you hear me, Nigel?"

"I hear you, Lil. But I can't answer the questions you're asking me."

"Nigel, this isn't a secret between you and Barney now. Think about it. Someone else knows, and that's why Barney killed himself."

Lillian was right. Without a doubt, the person who had mailed the manila envelope knew.

"You have a major exclusive that is sure to go national, and I can't believe you're letting it slip through your hands. Nigel? Nigel, are you listening to me?"

The siren faded and I imagined watching the emergency medical technicians race into Barney's house. I could picture their shifting faces when they rushed into the library and saw Barney slumped over in the wicker chair. The tall one with the impassive air would turn around, bolt outside, and vomit in the hedges. I was surprised. He had to have worked scenes like this before; he didn't look like a rookie. His co-worker, who looked ten or so years younger than him, walked right up to Barney. He could tell by looking that Barney had been dead for nearly an hour. He knelt beside the wicker chair. The disenchanted gaze in his eyes labeled him as one of the inspired. He had seen Barney on television and in newspaper photos. He had even met and shook hands with Barney at the city's Juneteenth celebration last week. He had believed in Barney's vision for a new, more progressive Florida, and he was going to make it known at the voting booth. And then I imagined watching him scratch his head as his eyes combed the room searching for Barney's shoes.

My brother, Caleb, and I lived on Circle Drive, a busy two-lane road a few blocks south of Apalachee Parkway and the state Capitol. Our house sat on a small almond-shaped bluff about forty yards from Circle Drive. Mammoth oaks, posing sycamores, and high-hat magnolias enshrouded the entire neighborhood under a canopy of trunk-size limbs and evergreen foliage.

We moved to Tallahassee and into 207 Circle Drive nine years ago. I arrived here in late July; two weeks after a phone interview with Russell landed me my first professional reporting job at the *Capitol Sentinel.* Caleb and I both thought it was best if he stayed in Richmond until I found our new home.

A realtor showed me the red brick house on the second day of my search. The house was more than perfect. Its physical features were not at the top of our requirements list. We were more concerned about the surroundings. Across the street from our house was Myers Park, a municipal recreation complex with baseball fields, basketball and tennis courts, a playground, and a web of scenic hiking and jogging trails. The neighbors were mostly retired and mid-career college professors and state bureaucrats, the kind of neighbors who kept to themselves or they're too busy to bother us. And then there's the narrow creek that snaked through the neighborhood and bound our back yard. When I saw the creek, I knew that this house could be our new home.

We brought the black leather recliner and nearly all of the furniture in the house with us when we moved here from our childhood home in Virginia. We packed what was left of our old life in a U-Haul and carted it into this life. The recliner sits by the living room window just as it had before. The framed family portraits hang on the living room and hallway walls in the same order. Neither of us smoked, but Dad's ashtrays were stationed at their usual posts throughout the house. Mom's sewing room and the family's home office shared the den to the right of the living room. There were still three bedrooms: mine, Caleb's, and our parents' bedroom.

Caleb was in his usual place when I arrived home from work: sitting in Dad's recliner, staring out the living room window, waiting anxiously for me. I spotted him before I turned into the driveway. When he saw me, a smile galloped across his face. I tried to hide my eyes from his scrutinizing gaze as I got out the car, but it was to no avail. Despair trailed me like a shadow, so Caleb knew something was wrong. He harnessed his smile, then retreated to his bedroom and sealed the door shut.

I used my key to unlock the front door. I took a deep breath before turning the doorknob, opening the door wide enough to squeeze inside.

The door slammed shut behind me.

As soon as Caleb heard the front door close, he emerged from his bedroom and asked, "So, how was our day?" I wanted to respond but Caleb's prying gaze unnerved me. I felt naked, exposed. "Don't tell me it was that bad," he solicited. His gaze followed me as I walked over to the sofa and sat down. He sat in the black recliner and extended the leg rest. "We went to work this morning and…" he initiated.

This was the story of our life. I went out each day and brought back bits and pieces of the world. Then I gave the fragments to Caleb and he reconfigured them into a world that he could live in: a tangential world outside the walls, windows, and doors of 207 Circle Drive. This was our life.

CHAPTER 2 ✦ CALEB

I am Caleb. If you didn't know me and Nigel and saw us on the street, you'd probably assume we were brothers because of the resemblance. We have the same bronzed complexion. We sport tight fades. And we both have our dad's tight-lipped smile. When I was a little boy, I looked like Dad. At least I did in the pictures that hung on the wall in the hallway. Nigel looked like Mom and Dad. He had a round face like Mom. Mine was more chiseled like Dad's. Nigel had a polished, intellectual air, while my look was more raw and natural. Don't get me wrong; I was not thug raw. I was straight-up, in-your-face. And I was about three inches taller than Nigel, who had bow legs that were partially straightened by metal braces that he wore until he was nine. I was three so I don't remember Nigel in braces, but I'd seen pictures of him wearing them. I used to tease him about his curvaceous legs. "If you let me iron those legs of yours straight," I cajoled him, "you'd be tall as Shaq." He stopped forcing smiles at that joke six years ago. It never garnered a laugh.

The morning after Barney died, Nigel saw the *Sentinel*'s front-page headline, *Reporter Tried to Stop Shooting.* He didn't say a word; he simply laid the newspaper on the sofa before he got up and closed the curtains and unplugged the phone. Barney's death sent the news media into a frenzy. I expected reporters and photographers to swarm like bees over Circle Drive. I spent the day sitting at the window, sneaking peeks out the curtains. I waited on the news trucks and satellites parade, which evidently, was rerouted at the last minute. Not a single one showed up, which pissed me off. I was ready for my fifteen minutes. I didn't tell Nigel, but that night I plugged the phone back up. We were eating breakfast the next morning when the phone rang. Nigel almost blew a gasket.

"Why is the phone ringing?" Nigel asked as he stared directly at me.

"Could it be that someone's calling?" I answered with a light-hearted grin.

"But, why do we hear it ringing?" he inquired.

Still trying to make light of the situation, I pointed at my ears. "Hello, we have these."

Evidently, he didn't get where I was coming from.

"I was joking, Nigel," I said. "Come on, man. Lighten up." I eyed Nigel cautiously as I answered the phone.

Before I could say hello, the caller announced, "This is Richard Aman. May I speak with Nigel Greene?"

I knew Richard Aman was Barney's father, so I responded, "Mr. Aman, I'm Nigel's brother, Caleb, and I want to let you know that you have my condolences. Barney was a great guy."

"Thank you, Caleb," Richard replied.

"Here's Nigel," I said and handed Nigel the phone. I sat next to Nigel on the sofa and listened to his part of the conversation.

"This is Nigel."

"Mr. Aman, I'm glad you called."

"Yes, sir."

"You're right. I'd only known Barney for a short time, but long enough to know that he was a great guy."

"Of course."

"We'll stop by tomorrow."

After hanging up with Richard Aman, but before he could turn off the ringer, the phone rang again. It was Lillian. She called to tell Nigel he had received several interview requests, but she informed everyone that he was unavailable. And that's when I discovered why our fifteen minutes never came. Lillian had been gatekeeping.

The next day, Nigel changed the phone number to an unlisted one.

As far back as I could remember, Nigel had been a passive observer. He always had the ability to detach from everything around him— to become unaffected. That didn't mean he wasn't compassionate. Nigel was the most caring person I knew. If you needed him, he'd be there. But you had to let him know you needed him because he probably wouldn't realize it on his own.

Nigel could be charming too. At least he could when he wanted to be. And when he's not trying, he could even be funny. Most of all, Nigel was thoughtful. If you asked anyone who knew him, they'd tell you that they considered him a good friend. But if you listened closely for what they didn't say, you'd realize that none of them really knew him. It's not their fault, though. Nigel never let anyone inside our world. We didn't have any real friends and no one ever called or stopped by to visit.

That's why I didn't get Nigel's stressing about Barney Aman. Nigel got more than a little pissed off when I agreed with Lillian. Barney's death was our ticket to the big-time. We had an exclusive that could've taken us places, and he walked away from it.

When we "met" Barney, I saw a reflection of two men. It was something about his restrained manner—the practiced way he carried himself. Nigel saw Barney's regal demeanor as a product of his privileged upbringing, but I thought he was way too put together. The man you saw when you met Barney was the sculpted façade he wanted you to see. This sculpted façade became even more gouging as Barney the Candidate marched toward the governor's office.

It didn't take very long for me to realize there was more to Barney than what we had seen when we met him at his campaign headquarters the day after he declared his candidacy. Barney had never held an elected office, so his candidacy came as a surprise to the media, the political arena, and to everyone who knew Barney. However, his impeccably furnished headquarters on Monroe Street, a few blocks from the Capitol, and his high-profile staff challenged what he described as, "...waking up a few mornings ago consumed by an urgent need to enter politics." In my mind, Barney was so full of it.

Waiting for us in the downstairs lobby was Eddie Johnson, a cartoonish man recognized more for his laughable efforts to hide his balding head beneath an assortment of outlandish toupees than for his political savvy. At five-five and 160 pounds, Eddie didn't look like the kind of man who could craft the campaigns of three incumbent congressmen—two in the House, one in the Senate. Eddie laid out Barney's political stance as he led us up the stairs to Barney's office. The door was open, so we walked right in.

Barney was outside on the patio, overlooking Monroe Street. As soon as Eddie walked out the office and closed the door, Barney breezed inside like the wind carried him. He closed the French doors, stepped off a cloud, and walked up to us. He served a warm, transparent smile. "Hi. I'm Barney Aman, Florida's next governor." Nigel and I thought Barney's dramatic entrance was scripted, and that was the last thing we agreed on.

Nigel never saw Barney's reflection. At least he pretended not to see the reflection of a man Barney kept locked away, hidden from prying eyes. The public, including Nigel, was captivated by Barney and clamored to hear every carefully chosen word that rolled off his tongue. They watched his every move. I found it hard to believe that only three people saw Barney's reflection: me, Barney, and the woman who armed a manila envelope marked, *Deliver to Addressee Only*, with a copy of her husband's death certificate and a news clipping describing his suspicious death and mailed it to Nigel.

Nigel worried too much about things that had nothing to do with our life. For the past three days, he'd been sitting in front of the television watching The Weather Channel non-stop. He left earlier today to go by Richard Aman's office, but as soon as he walked back in the door, he plopped down on the sofa and turned the television to The Weather Channel. Tonight, a two-hour documentary about Alaska premiered on The Weather Channel. After the documentary went off, Nigel began agonizing over weather in the frozen state even though we lived in sunny Florida. "It's unseasonably warm in Alaska," he turned and said, "and scientists are starting to worry." I didn't have the heart to say it, but I couldn't stop the look in my eyes from screaming, *I don't give a damn*. Nigel didn't see my nonchalance as a sign of disinterest. Instead, he saw a blank canvas on which he could paint a much more detailed image. "Global warming is one of the biggest issues facing the world today," he sketched. I pretended to listen. Pretending to listen isn't as easy as it appears, but I've mastered the technique. It takes a lot of practice to get it right. I started by looking—not staring—in his general direction. Staring can give you away. "Scientists have determined that the polar caps are melting," Nigel continued to draw. "Did you know that?" Unconsciously, I detected a pause in his voice so I nodded slightly. It wasn't a yes or no nod, but more of a maybe nod. "If the polar caps continue to melt at the rate they are melting now…"

I heard Nigel, but I wasn't listening to him because there were things much closer to home to worry about. I was about to go crazy wondering what we're going to do now that he'd quit our job. We're not broke, so money wasn't the problem. We had enough saved and invested to live comfortably for the rest of our life. The real problem was these walls. Nigel would never admit it, but he would much rather stay here and hide out than to be part of the world out there. He ventured out since I couldn't. He's my link to everything outside these walls. His life was my life, so, if Nigel didn't have a job to go to, then we didn't have a life outside this house. This was it.

Even though I couldn't make myself step outside this house, it didn't mean something's wrong with me. I used to tell myself that on a daily basis, but these days, the only time I had to remind myself of this was when I'd been shut up in this house for too long. It'd only been a couple of days, so I didn't have to convince myself of my sanity, at least not yet. What's scary to me was the knowledge that Nigel wasn't interested in looking for another job right now, and I didn't know when he would be interested. That meant I could expect day after day and week after week of being surrounded by these walls. That's enough to make a person go crazy.

Three years ago, after I'd had a very bad Monday morning, I found a way to establish my own connection to the world outside these walls. It was via a blog, "The (not so true) Way I Remember It." Funny, huh? Well, that was the point. I didn't want to bring people into my claustrophobic world; I wanted to be out there with them and to be part of their world. And then, I wanted, no, needed a little humor in my life. The blog had been successful on both accords. I had almost 25,000 subscribers, and every now and then, I got to laugh until I cracked up about the fun-filled life I pretended to have lived.

Once a week, I wrote and posted a blog about the way life used to be back in the day. Or at least the way I imagined I would re-member life back then if I could. Sometimes, the columns reflected nostalgically about the good times I was sure we had growing up in the '80s and '90s, while others reflected earnestly on the triumphs and the tragedies that were seemingly connected like Siamese twins to everyone's life. It's no secret to my subscribers that the memories I wrote about were made up. I was upfront about my memory loss and admitted that I didn't remember anything about my life prior to waking up from a coma eleven years ago, so they knew that I juxtaposed myself into these tales of an unforgettable childhood and the good ol' days. Judging from the comments to the blog, it has touched a lot of people out there. I took the wild guess that they were touched since, although I probably never lived any of the memories that I wrote about, deep inside my heart, I felt like I had.

I'm sure Nigel read the blog, but he'd never mentioned anything about it.

Another job wasn't the only thing Nigel didn't show an interest in. He'd never been much of a talker, which wasn't a problem since I talked enough for both of us. But, except when he's going on about the weather, Nigel hadn't said much at all. I'd practically tried to reach inside him and pull out conversations on several occasions. I had to be careful, though. If I pulled too hard or too often, he'd retreat to his bedroom and leave me out here talking to myself.

This was me talking to myself. I didn't have anyone else to talk to because Nigel didn't bother to get out of bed today. He'd been shut up in his bedroom all day. I was not stressing about it though. I talked to my-self all the time, mostly to say things that I couldn't say to Nigel; words that I had to speak out loud, if only in my mind, since thoughts weren't real until they are verbalized or lived.

I imagined how it must feel to run. I couldn't remember ever running, but as I gazed out the window at people jogging around Myers Park, the freedom of unbridled motion resurrected my soul. I started running. My heart raced as I accelerated and challenged the wind, overtaking time. I was running. Running. Running until I slammed head-on into these walls. My trepidation and these unyielding walls were formidable hurdles.

We hadn't been to the grocery store since two weeks before Barney died. So tonight's dinner, like last night's and the night before that, was whatever I could scrape together. There were six cans of minestrone soup, two cans of green peas, and a can of corned beef in the cabinet. Two ice trays had the freezer to themselves. A pitcher of water and a bowl of minestrone soup Nigel had for lunch fought for space in the refrigerator. The rice container was half full. And we'd given out of sugar three days ago.

"How does corned beef and rice sound?" I asked Nigel.

Instead of responding, Nigel sat there contemplating whether he wanted corned beef and rice or something else. Why? It wasn't like he was gonna get off his sorry ass and go get anything else.

"Nigel, we have six cans of minestrone soup, a can of corned beef, two cans of green peas, and a cup of rice," I informed him as I walked into the living room. "The menu's either corned beef and rice or more minestrone soup."

"Corned beef and rice," Nigel suggested, then stood up and turned off the ceiling fan. He sat back down, picked up the TV remote, and changed the channel.

"Thank God," I said. "I was starting to see *Locals On The 8s* in my sleep."

As I walked back to the kitchen Nigel announced, "We'll go to the store tomorrow."

"Okay," I acknowledged with a guilty smile. "I'll make out a shopping list tonight."

Nigel hated minestrone soup. I was not that crazy about it either, but I kept it in stock for times like this.

It was almost 3 a.m. and I was in bed, pretending to sleep. I know it's kind of crazy to pretend to sleep when you're the only person in the room, but my reason was a good one, which exempted me from the crazy label. Sleep didn't always come easy for me, and it's due to these dreams that I kept having. Tonight, before I woke up, I dreamed that Nigel and I were at a beach swimming, but the beach was inside this house. Last night, I dreamed we were at a concert, but the concert was in the living room. Every night, it's a different dream, but we're always inside this house. I pretended sleep so I could pretend to dream of being outside...anywhere outside.

Barbed wire. That's what these walls were made of. From ceiling to floor, floor to ceiling. Barbed wire brandished millions of dutiful razors sharp enough to deli-slice flesh, memories, and hope.

I wanted to hate Barney Aman for taking the easy way out. I wanted to hate him because Nigel was unemployed, which meant we didn't exist outside this house. More than anything, I wanted to hate him for unearthing the memory of the rueful Monday morning three years ago when I tried to abandon our life. But I couldn't.

CHAPTER 3 ✧

The last Thursday in June turned out to be a day of firsts. The day began with a cluster of fugitive clouds, bringing the summer's first rain. It was only eight days into the summer, but after three months of breathing stale, dusty air and toasting in a sweltering heat wave, the scattered showers were graciously welcomed by closed umbrellas.

For the first time in Richard Aman's well-documented life, he tried to elude the spotlight when he stepped outside the doors of First Baptist Church. There was nowhere for him to hide from the squadron of reporters, including Lillian, or the roguish lenses seizing him from every angle as he trailed his son's mahogany coffin. Today, he was not the charismatic political icon who skillfully used the media to make sure he never lost an election in his forty-five-year career. Today, he was the grieving parent of a man who took his own life. He was a father standing at his son's grave while a woman with an operatic voice sang a stirring version of "Amazing Grace." He was a man living a day that was not supposed to be part of his life. And he wondered if anyone really saw him.

A woman with doleful eyes stood off from the mourners and spectators gathered at Springhill Cemetery. She poked the ground with the tip of her orange and green umbrella as the drizzling rain soaked through her black dress and low-heeled black pumps. She was one of the inspired. She became a crusader. She tacked flyers on street poles, taped them on store windows, and passed them out at local housing projects. She even organized a voter registration drive. And today, for the first time in her life, the woman, Karen, cried for a man she never met.

Today was a first for another woman who no one noticed. It wasn't that they didn't see her; they did. But to them, she was simply another lamentable face in the montage of mourners. They didn't see her eyes dart back and forth between the flower-draped coffin and the man standing behind Richard Aman. That man was Nigel Greene, who attended the funeral at the personal request of Richard Aman. Nigel saw the woman staring at him, and although it was the first time he'd seen her, he knew that the woman was Frances Pelt. And Nigel knew that she was feeling something she'd felt only once before—the world shifting under her feet.

"I'm sorry," Nigel said under his breath to Frances.

Frances had hoped that Nigel wouldn't be at the funeral because, unlike everyone else, Nigel knew why Barney fled. Barney may have pulled the trigger that ended his life, but it was an angry phone call from a dejected lover three nights earlier that loaded the black pistol and a manila envelope armed with a death certificate and newspaper clipping that pointed the barrel at Barney's head. Frances knew the kindly man mouthing the words, "I'm sorry," was Nigel and recognition was something she didn't want. She turned to run, but her feet could not find traction on the mutating earth. Before she realized it, she was on her hands and knees. Frances tried to will herself to get up, but her soul questioned why. Until nine months ago, when Richard Aman and a gang of political bigwigs told Barney they were going to make him Florida's next governor, Frances shared a life with Barney's reflection. For nine years, they lived in a veiled world that Barney actualized. After her husband's death, Frances resented the boundaries Barney set for their relationship even more, but not enough to stop loving him. She still loved him. And she knew Barney loved her, too. After all, it was Barney who made her believe love was love whether shared during the pyramidal hours of life or amid the ephemeral twinkling of dreams. But today, when it didn't matter at all, she felt free to express her love—free to not care how many eyebrows were raised or fingers and umbrellas pointed. There was no reason to care. So she lay on the ground beside Barney's grave and waited to be buried.

Firsts were few and next to none in Nigel's life, but, when he walked over to Frances and extended his hand, he sensed something was about to happen to him that had never happened before.

"Barney died," Nigel told Frances. "Not you." Frances looked up at Nigel but quickly turned away. "Take my hand," Nigel offered. "Please." Frances' body shook as she placed her muddied hand in Nigel's.

Suddenly, the rain stopped falling on Nigel and Frances. He looked up and saw Karen holding her umbrella over them. "Thanks," Nigel said. Karen put her arm around Frances as Nigel helped her stand as the three of them made their way through the inquisitive stares, the earsplitting whispers, the probing camera lenses, and the wrought iron gates of Springhill Cemetery.

As soon as the gates were behind them and the sidewalk gave Frances a momentary foothold on the shifting earth, she turned to Nigel and Karen and said, "Thank you. I can make it from here."

"Are you sure you're okay?" Karen asked. "Are you parked nearby?" Before Frances could reply, she suggested, "It's raining. Let me walk you to your car."

"That's okay. I'm parked right up the street." Frances mustered a grateful smile. "I'll be fine."

Nigel turned to Karen. "Thanks for helping out."

"Just doing my part," Karen responded with a thoughtful smile. "God bless."

Nigel watched as she closed her umbrella and walked away without bothering to look back or even glance over her shoulder. It's good she didn't. If she had, she would've seen the motley look on Nigel's face when he turned to say good-bye to Frances and found proof. Frances got in a blue Bonneville parked on the curb. A Bonneville with a Duval County tag. Duval County includes Jacksonville. A Jacksonville postmark was stamped on the manila envelope. Proof that Frances mailed the envelope, and validation that she helped pulled the trigger.

There were more firsts that day.

Nigel had been driving since he was seventeen, but suddenly he could not remember how to crank the car and drive away from the cemetery. The keys were in his hands, but he didn't know what to do with them. After the woman whose name he didn't know disappeared and Frances drove away, Nigel walked across the street to where he was parked a few spaces down from where Frances had been parked. He unlocked the car door, got in, and closed the door. He sat there staring at the keys in his hand, wishing he could drive away from the memory of being at a similar-looking cemetery thirteen years ago.

Nigel had not stepped inside a cemetery since his parents were buried. He knew attending Barney's funeral would mean having to relive that day thirteen years ago, so he wasn't surprised when the memory of that day met him at the gate. As he walked inside the wrought iron gates of Springhill Cemetery, he remembered his uncle, Walter, and his aunt, Girlie, standing beside him as he stared at his mother's and father's coffins. His cousin Jerry and his wife, Frankie, stood behind him. He could still feel the loneliness he felt that day because Caleb was in a coma at a hospital four blocks from the cemetery and couldn't be there to say goodbye to their parents.

Nigel managed to cloud the memories of that day by focusing on Richard Aman and Frances during Barney's funeral and burial. But now, sitting alone in his car with the keys in his hands, the memories would not let him think of anything else. He remembered staring into the distance to avoid looking at the two flower-draped coffins. Snow covered the cemetery, which strangely made it appear more inviting. A trio of birds playfully hopped from one headstone to another. An elderly man placed flowers on the snow at the base of a headstone, then he seemed to have found something to smile about. Nigel remembered hearing the preacher speaking, but he couldn't recall anything that he had said. His uncle's arm was around him. His aunt leaned over on him; her tears soaked the jacket of his suit. He remembered the last words his mother had said to him, "Take care of your brother."

"Caleb," he said out loud to vanquish the memories and to remind himself that Caleb was home waiting for him. Nigel took a few deep breaths as he ushered the past back to its proper place. Then, he put the key in the ignition, cranked the car, and drove away.

CHAPTER 4 ✧ CALEB

That night saw another first.

I was sitting in Dad's recliner by the window when Nigel pulled in the driveway. I waited until Nigel got out the car before I went to my bedroom and closed the door. When I heard the front door open and close, I walked out of my bedroom and asked, "How was our day?" Without responding, Nigel marched through the living room, squeezed by me in the hallway, and retreated to his bedroom. "Was it that bad?" I asked.

It wasn't the first time Nigel had come home and locked up in his bedroom without saying a word. He's done it several times before. I usually got upset when Nigel didn't want to share his day. But, I wasn't mad on this day of firsts because I was aware our day was spent burying a man whose death changed our lives.

It was Thursday and I cooked pork chops like I do every Thursday. Today, it was stuffed pork chops. Last Thursday, it was fried pork chops. The week before that, grilled pork chops. And the Thursday before that, baked pork chops covered with tomatoes and onions. So, pork chops for dinner on Thursday wasn't a first, nor was eating dinner in the living room while watching *Wheel of Fortune* and *Jeopardy*. Both were part of our Thursday night routine.

I placed the last dish in the dishwasher, turned it on, then walked in the living room where Nigel had the remote in his hand channel surfing.

"Richard Aman lives in a gated section of Charleston Estates," Nigel said before he laid the remote on the sofa beside him. "There's a guard shack at the entrance. Maybe, I shouldn't call it a shack. It's almost as big as our house."

My eyes lit up. I raced across the living room and jumped in the recliner.

"Richard wanted us to ride in the limo with him, but I told him we'd rather drive our car because we had an appointment after the funeral," Nigel recounted.

"What kind of appointment?" I asked.

"There wasn't an appointment," Nigel responded. "I told him that to keep from riding in the limo. Anyway, we followed the limo to First Baptist Church,"

As Nigel continued recounting our day, I stared at the ceiling and imagined that Nigel and I were walking out the doors of First Baptist Church behind Richard Aman and a mahogany coffin. We lowered our heads and placed our hands in front of our faces to avoid Lillian's apathetic stare and the barrage of cameras lenses closing in on us. The scene shifted, and we now stood behind Richard Aman at Springhill Cemetery. A woman sang an operatic version of "Amazing Grace" while another woman that no one noticed drowned in her tears. Her name was Frances Pelt, and the earth was shifting beneath Frances' feet. She tried to run but she slipped and fell on the ground beside Barney's grave. Frances had forgotten she was alive, so we walked over to Frances and let her know she wasn't dead. We led her past the stares and whispers, through the wrought-iron gates, to a blue Bonneville parked on the curb a block away. We waved bye as Frances began the lonely and regretful journey back to her dispirited life in Jacksonville. Nigel's day became my day.

Nigel pulled the remote out from between the sofa pillows, then turned to The Weather Channel. For eleven years, since I came home from the hospital, Nigel's life had been my life. But that night, for the first time, Nigel swallowed the acrid guilt curdling in his mouth and selfishly kept the woman whose name he didn't know to himself.

CHAPTER 5 ✦ NIGEL

Caleb was trying to make me get out of bed. That's why he and Tupac were in the living room headlining a concert for the entire neighborhood. I must have lucked out and won a front-row ticket. My head, like my house shoes which were on the floor beside the bed, tap danced as the walls, floor, and ceiling palpitated to a thunderous bass that suffocated Caleb's and Pac's vocals.

Yesterday, it was Caleb and Will Smith. That spectacle started around seven-thirty with Caleb bellowing "Brothers Just Don't Understand," his version of Smith's ode to parental cluelessness. It ended at four minutes 'til ten when I was tired of hearing them "Gettin' Jiggy Wit It." I jumped out of bed, charged out the room, and stumbled over Caleb, who was in the hallway spinning, kicking, and grabbing his crotch.

"That move was Michael's," I yelled, "not Will's!"

Caleb saw the anger in my eyes and he knew where I was headed. He tried to hold me down to keep me from getting up. Dragging him behind me, I crawled into the living room and over to the front door. I reached up and grabbed the doorknob, then yanked the front door open. I let the world inside. Caleb took off to his bedroom and I closed the door and locked it. I unplugged the CD player, the television, the phone and the answering machine, everything that could make a sound. Then I went back to my bedroom, remade my bed, and hid under the covers until the sun began to set.

This morning's show started at seven-thirty. Around eight-thirty, Caleb and Pac were still performing songs from Pac's early years. I knew why Caleb was pissed off. That's why I lay in bed and promised not to say a word unless "Keep Your Head Up" was on his playlist. There was no way I was going to let him desecrate my favorite Pac song.

Memories were killing me. Not all memories...only the uninvited ones.

I tried not to think about Flatley Creek or the thin membrane of ice covering it that ominous December evening thirteen years ago, but it's getting harder and harder for me to choose which memories replay and when. Flatley Creek was a narrow but deep stream that bordered the backyard of the house we grew up in. The creek, a stone's throw from every house in the neighborhood, was about fifty feet across at its widest point and over seven feet deep in the middle. Caleb and I bought this house because the creek outside my window reminded me of Flatley Creek.

When I didn't want to see the creek outside my window, I closed the curtains and blinds. I was still searching for a shade that can obscure the memory of Flatley Creek on that ineffaceable winter evening. Closing my eyes doesn't work because the inside of my eyelids turn into Imax projection screens. Some nights the memories are so vivid that I have to tape my eyelids and sleep with my eyes wide open. The paper tape is loose enough for me to blink but too tight for my eyes to stay closed. I used regular tape for a while, but after a few nights, I looked kind of funny without any eyebrows or lashes.

Caleb was able to forget that December night and everything about our life before that night. He didn't have to deal with the tragedy because he slipped into a coma and was spared the heart-break of knowing what had transpired. Every day, I sat next to Caleb's bed and prayed for him to wake up. I was relieved when he didn't. When he awoke from the coma two years and six days later, he was diagnosed with psychogenic amnesia. His entire life had been erased. He didn't know who he was or who I was. And he didn't ask about Mom or Dad. He never even questioned why he was in the hospital. Two weeks passed before Uncle Walter and I told him that Mom and Dad were dead. We didn't tell him how they died because his eyes were uninhabited, which meant it was hard to gauge his response to the knowledge that they were dead.

Why was I remembering this?

I was by his side every waking moment for several weeks after he came out of the coma. At first, we barely spoke, which in hindsight was a good thing because I didn't know what to say to him. When we did converse, it was because I had asked a question or made a comment and he responded.

That was also when we discovered that Caleb had developed an acute case of agoraphobia. His fear of the world outside the hospital room was virulently crippling. He couldn't even stand to be in the room with the windows open, so, the loss of his memory was the least of our problems. However, it turned out that his memory loss was an asset when it came time to move on with our life. We were both starting with a clean slate. I wasn't sure how I was going to make our new life work, but I knew I had to find a way to take care of Caleb and to help him move into our new life.

Three weeks after Caleb woke up from the coma, his doctors felt he was ready to be released. They suggested that Caleb and I both seek counseling to help us deal with the emotional impact of the past two years, but neither of us thought counseling was necessary. However, when it came time for us to leave the hospital, Caleb became extremely anxious. When I asked him what was wrong, he said he was nervous because he couldn't remember his life before the accident, which meant he had no idea what life was like outside of his hospital room. I assured him that life was no different outside the hospital and he calmed down. An hour before we left the hospital, doctors sedated Caleb so that an ambulance could transport him home. Uncle Walter and Aunt Girlie were against us moving back into our parents' house, but we moved in anyway.

When Caleb woke up in his bedroom at our parents' house, he lay in bed staring around at his unfamiliar surroundings. He knew he was in his bedroom at our parents' house, but he could not remember ever being there. He asked, "Where am I?"

"You're home," I answered.

"Home?" he asked.

"Our home."

A lasting vestige of that December night was my brother's inability to remember our life with Mom and Dad. He saw their pictures on the walls; sat in Dad's recliner every day; cooked in Mom's cast iron skillet; and thoroughly cleaned their bedroom once a year. He even wrote about them, well at least a made-up version of them, in a blog, "The (not so true) Way I Remember It." But to this day, neither one of us had ever said a word to each other about Mom or Dad.

The woman I met at Barney's funeral had become my guilty pleasure. I didn't know her name or anything about her, but I could still hear her saying, "Just doing my part." I could still see her graceful smile. Her brown eyes, they were mesmerizing. I was trying not to obsess about her, but it'd been a long time since I met someone I really wanted to get to know personally. For the past nine years, I'd been a journalist and the first rule of being a reporter was to remain objective. Stay outside the story and don't get too close to the people you're writing about. This rule, which I applied to my personal life, was never a problem. I didn't want to get too acquainted with anyone I interviewed or met. But it's not like that with her. I'd been dying to see her and to talk to her. I want to know who she is. Know her favorite color. Her favorite food. Her favorite song. I want to know what makes her smile. I really, really want to know what makes her smile. One day soon, I hope to know everything about her, but until then, I'll settle for just knowing her name.

Who am I hurting by keeping her to myself?
No one, I told my conscience.
Then, why am I keeping her a secret?
Because...
Because why?
...
You better be careful. Keeping secrets can be risky.
Shut the hell up, I cursed my conscience. You don't have to keep reminding me. I know how destructive secrets can be. But think about it this way. I'll probably never see her again. So what's the harm in keeping her a secret?
You're not hearing me. So go ahead and do what you want to do, my bedraggled conscience snapped back. Just don't say I didn't warn you.

Am I being selfish by keeping her to myself? I've pondered this question nearly every hour since I met her. So far I've been able to justify keeping her to myself and not sharing her with Caleb.

I'd convinced myself that he doesn't need to know about her because I don't know anything about her. However, the real reason I think I've kept her a secret has to do with how desperate I've become since I met her. There's no way I want to share this asthmatic feeling with my brother.

It was Sunday afternoon and I'd been in bed all day. Caleb had been doing something in the den most of the day. The den was divided into our home office and Mom's sewing room. Neither of us sews, so the only time either of us go on that side of the den was when Caleb steps over there to dust the sewing machine and change the faded spool of black thread during his spring cleaning frenzy. Now, the office was mainly used when Caleb wrote his blog, but we used to use it when I brought home interview notes so Caleb could write articles for the newspaper under my byline.

When I got up to get a drink of water around noon, Caleb had already prepared lunch: slaw dogs on toasted buns and baked beans. He was sitting at the desk working on the computer. I figured he was working on a new blog. I still was not sure how I felt about Caleb writing this blog. I knew it gave him something to do, but I didn't think it's a good idea for him to make up memories about our childhood. Caleb looked up and saw me, and I nodded toward the door. He got up and went to his bedroom, and I went outside to get Saturday's and Sunday's *Capitol Sentinel* out of the delivery box. When I got back inside, I fixed two slaw dogs and a large bowl of baked beans and went in the living room. The television was off, so I didn't bother to turn it on. I didn't read the newspapers either. I haven't since my photo appeared in the sidebar story to the article about Barney's suicide. I sat there eating and periodically glancing at Caleb who was working diligently at whatever he was doing.

"What are you doing?" I finally broke down and asked, "Working on your blog?"

"No," he answered. "I'm not doing anything."

"You look a little too busy to..."

Caleb cut me off. "Can't talk right now."

Without saying a word, I walked in the kitchen, put the plate in the sink, then went to my bedroom. The blinds and curtains in the bedroom were still closed and the light was off, so the room was lit by shadows. I'd never been able to sleep in an unmade bed, so I pulled the blanket, sheets and pillows off the bed. I shook the sheets and placed them back on the bed, making sure to tuck all four corners of the sheet under the top mattress. I spread the blanket across the bed and straightened it. Then I fluffed the four pillows. When I was done, I turned back the blanket, took off my slides, and climbed in bed. And that was where I spent the rest of the day.

It was a little past midnight when Caleb finally went to bed. There was a stack of manila envelopes and letters on the desk in the den. The eight letters, all printed on beige linen paper, were cover letters attached to copies of my resume, also on linen paper. There was a note for me clipped to the letters. Caleb wanted me to sign the letters. "Make sure you sign them as Dr. Nigel Greene." I earned my Ph.D. years ago, but I'd never referred to myself as Dr. Greene.

Caleb had already purchased metered postage stamps online, so the envelopes were stamped and addressed to potential employers. Three were for public relations jobs. One was for a radio show host position at Tallahassee's talk radio station. Two were addressed to the advertising and marketing departments of a media consulting firm. Florida A & M University had two openings. One was for an assistant professor of journalism and the other was for a communications specialist. Caleb completed the university's employment application and attached it to the letters and resumes. The last letter was addressed to Richard Aman's Tallahassee-based Aman Realty, one of the largest privately owned real estate companies in Florida.

I met Richard Aman two days after Barney killed himself. Mr. Aman called and asked me if I could stop by his office after lunch. I didn't want to go, but Caleb talked me into going. After meeting Mr. Aman, I was glad I went. The first words he said to me when I walked into his office and closed the door were, "Thank you." The police had given him a copy of Barney's suicide note, the content of which, surprisingly, was never publicized. Because of the note and the TV and newspaper headlines, Mr. Aman knew I had spoken with Barney right before his death, and he assumed I knew why Barney shot himself.

"I don't want to know what my son was hiding," he said. "I simply want to thank you for trying to help him, and for refusing to take part in dismantling my son's life." He motioned for me to sit in a brown leather chair in front of his sprawling cherry oak desk. "I'm forever indebted to you, Mr. Greene."

"I was only doing what I thought was right," I responded.

"Well, there aren't too many people today who feel that way," Richard said with a warm smile. "I'm glad it was you covering the story."

I smiled and tried to stop myself from squirming in the chair.

Richard continued. "You're a good man, Mr. Greene, and I want to show my appreciation by offering you a job since you quit yours."

"Thanks," I said. "But, can you give me a little time to think about it?"

"Sure," he replied. "Take all the time you need."

I knew Caleb was desperate for me to get a job because he included the letter to Aman Realty. During the past month, we'd only gone out three times. We stopped by Richard Aman's office. Attended the funeral of a man we hardly knew, and went to the grocery store. So he's starving for a life outside this house.

Since Caleb took the time to conduct a job search, type a resume and cover letters, go online and pay for postage, and then address all the envelopes, I decided to sign seven of the letters. The other—a cover letter and resume for Aman Realty—ended up in the wastebasket. I appreciated Mr. Aman's offer, but I didn't turn away from Barney's story and quit my job at the newspaper because I needed anyone's gratitude. I did it because I sympathized with Barney, who I believed was living a tragically flawed life. Barney's flaw was trying to live in two worlds with intersecting orbits. In one world, Barney was the privileged son of an iconic politician and wealthy businessman. In the other, a private world he created, he was a man desperately trying to appease his kept lover whose husband died four years ago in a suspicious accident the night he found out about their affair. Barney thought ending the relationship before he began his bid for governor was the only way to keep his two worlds apart. He must have been blind not to see the collision ahead.

Most people die without ever living their own lives because their lives belong to everyone who was part of their world. My life belonged to Caleb.

I took three sleeping pills, but they didn't help. I had been lying in bed for three hours dreaming even though I was wide awake. I wished I could reset the hands on the clock and fast forward to sunrise since, most of the time, daylight could chase the dream away with the dark. The dream, which kept repeating itself, was a familiar dream. In the dream, I was standing on the banks of a narrow, winding creek that bordered the back yard of a two-story, red-brick house. It was cold. Freezing cold. And snowing. Even though night was settling in, I could see a thin sheet of ice crystallizing on the surface of the embittered creek. That's when the dream ended, but only long enough to rewind and begin again.

A couple of months ago, I asked Caleb did he ever dream.

"That's a dumb-ass question," he snapped. "Everybody dreams."

"What I meant to ask was, in your dreams...?" I hesitated.

"In my dreams...what?"

"Are you outside...or...?"

"...or still trapped inside here?" Caleb finished for me. He turned and looked out the front window. Little Leaguers, and their coaches, parents and fans were getting ready for the regional championship game at Myers Park. A group of young men were playing a game of full-court basketball. The tennis courts were filled. And joggers and hikers appeared and disappeared on the park's meandering trails. "No," Caleb answered and pointed out the window at Myers Park. "In my dreams, I'm not trapped inside of this house. I'm out there."

I'd give anything to dream I was in Myers Park instead of standing on the banks of Flatley Creek in the cold.

We lived cloistered lives that paled in comparison to the lives of people like Barney Aman. Two months after Barney's death, his story still made headlines and dominated the evening news. I knew Caleb and I will not be missed when our life ends, but I worried whether anyone would know we ever existed.

CHAPTER 6 ✧ CALEB

Nigel told me to pick up a book and read it since I was so obviously bored. "I will as soon as you climb out of the fairytale world you're wallowing in," I shot back. Nigel's eyes immediately became interim ice-picks that he used to stab me twice in the neck. I deserved it though, because I never told Nigel why I let my library card expire or why I no longer had a passion for reading. What he didn't realize was, when I read and get to know characters in books, sometimes I become overwhelmed by a morose sympathy for these people whose destiny was to live lives, happy or sad, in compassed worlds akin to mine.

Three different gubernatorial campaign ads aired during the last hour's commercial breaks. Barney's death sent the gubernatorial campaign into high gear and the candidates began a soul-killing, but bloodless, battle for Barney's vacant frontrunner status. As I watched each candidate tout his attributes and point out the flaws of the competitors, I wondered if Barney would still be the front-runner if he hadn't killed himself. Would the secret he was running from have surfaced and knocked him out of the top spot and potentially out of the race?

Nigel wouldn't talk about Barney, and I understood why. Nigel had canonized Barney. In his mind, he'd made Barney into some-one heroic, someone inspiring. I guess there's nothing wrong with that if Barney really was a hero. I never saw Barney as the heroic type. How could he be a hero when he took the coward's way out? Had he stuck around longer, he may have become a hero because he really was one of the good guys. I surmised that Barney was a man who was too afraid to face his own questions about a night he couldn't remember. I sympathized with Barney's struggle because I'd been there too. And, unless you'd been there, you wouldn't know how hard it was to live in the present when you couldn't remember the past. It's like trying to go somewhere but not knowing how to get there because you didn't know where you started. The difference between us was I didn't let myself think about that day thirteen years ago. Barney could never move past the night he couldn't remember. He needed to know what happened on the night Frances Pelt's husband died under questionable circumstances. Whether or not Barney had anything to do with Terry Pelt's death, my guess was Richard Aman and his cohorts made any involvement Barney may have had disappear. He was in the clear. So, why couldn't Barney leave well enough alone?

"Do you think Barney had something to do with Terry Pelt's death?" I asked Nigel as we watched an ad attacking Clay Walton, who moved to the top of the polls after Barney's death. Before Nigel could respond, I answered my own question. "I think he did. Why would he kill himself if he didn't?"

That wasn't the first time I'd asked Nigel what he thought about Barney's death. But, unlike the other times, he decided to respond.

"According to the police reports, Terry was cleaning his rifle to go hunting the next day when it accidentally discharged," he explained.

"Terry was accidentally shot in the head, right?"

"Yes."

"And Barney deliberately shot himself in the head, right?"

"That's right," Nigel responded.

"Sounds like too much of a coincidence to me."

"The coroner's report established that Teddy's wound was more than likely an accident. And, could it be Barney killed himself because he was scared people would form false conclusions like you have?"

"If I knew I wasn't guilty of something, I wouldn't care how many false conclusions people came up with," I stated my position.

"Well, everyone isn't you," Nigel countered. "Some people worry about what others say and think about them. And there's nothing wrong with that. It simply means..." Nigel's voice trailed off as he began lecturing me.

I knew Nigel would go on forever about this. He hadn't talked this much in days, so I pretended I was listening. What I really wanted was for him to shut up, get off his ass, grab the car keys, and dip. He needed to go somewhere, anywhere, so we could get out of this house. Being locked up in this house for the past month and a half was driving me crazy, and it started to show on my face and in my conversations with him. I don't know why Nigel couldn't see how aggravated I was. Maybe he did, but pretended he didn't. But then, all of a sudden, Nigel's eyes tapered to razor slits and his eyebrows hovered like too taut bows. I figured he'd heard my thoughts. His voice palpitated as he said something I couldn't decipher. I nodded in congruence, but in my mind I screamed, "Get a life, Nigel!"

He must have heard me again because he stood and looked around the room. He turned off the ceiling fan, then continued looking around the living room for something. I hoped it was the car keys.

"What are you looking for?" I finally asked.

"The remote," Nigel answered. "I want to see what the weather's going to be like tomorrow."

I wanted to wring his neck.

I sat at the computer preparing to write a blog about Barney, when Nigel walked into the living room and saw me. He must have developed mind-reading skills because he looked right at me and said, "Do not write anything about Barney in your blog. Do you hear me, Caleb? Nothing." I usually get mad when Nigel talks to me like he's chastising a child because I'm a grown-ass man. I let it pass that time because it was the first time Nigel had ever mentioned the blog. However, he did give me an idea for a memory to write about.

The (not so true) Way I Remember It – by Caleb Greene
"How Momma Raised Good Children"

I hear it all the time.
Children are "badder" than they used to be.
I've heard it from relatives and friends who claim not to know where the children they're raising come from. I hear it from uncles and aunts, from people whose jobs require them to work with children, and from neighbors who live behind high fences or with bad dogs. And, after listening to them all complain about how bad children have become, they're caught off guard when I beg to differ.

My initial response to these people who are deliberately trying to give children a bad rap is what they're saying is an unproven fact. After explaining that an unproven fact is something you know to be true but only because your gut tells you it's true, I usually lay out my journalism credentials. You see, the first and most important lesson they teach future journalists at Richmond University is a factual error is an automatic failure. So, I learned to take issue with unproven facts.

However, most parents don't seem to care what they taught me or what I learned in college. I've read your comments and I know nothing short of divine intervention will convince most of you that children are not badder than they used to be.

I'm not sure who's to blame for starting this misconception about today's children, but I've come to the conclusion that the reason children appear to be badder than we used to be is because nowadays you can't tell children to "get lost." Or as my mother and father would command, "Get out of my sight and don't let me see you until I call for you."

On weekends, during the summer, or any time school was out, Nigel and I were literally thrown out the house. And some days, when they wanted us to be really good children, they didn't allow us to hang out in the yard.

By the time one of them walked out on the porch and yelled across three neighborhood blocks, the house would be cleaned, dinner would be cooked, and the only thing left to do was feed, bathe, and put their "good" children to bed.

The encroachment of society's seedy elements into neighborhoods has made it even more difficult for parents not to raise "bad" children. I'm sure no parent wants to put their children in harm's way and they shouldn't. But how can you raise "good" children if you can't tell them to get lost? Getting lost when told to do so is what made us good children.

Technology is also to blame.

When was the last time you told someone to get lost? And they did? Or could?

Technology won't allow people to get lost.

Back in the day, when you needed to talk to someone, your options were to call their house or yell across three neighborhood blocks. If they were home, good. If not, you yelled until you were hoarse or you called back every ten minutes until their mother took the phone off the hook and you got a busy signal for the next hour.

Today, if the person you need to speak with isn't home, you can probably reach them on their cell phone even if they're somewhere they shouldn't be talking on the phone, like in church or class. Most of today's so-called bad children have cell phones, which presents yet another problem. Even if you could tell them to get lost, you wouldn't have a hard enough time finding them. Just call your bad children's cell phones and yell, "Get here!"

After I finished the column, I was glad Nigel had told me not to write about Barney Aman. It was for a spiteful reason though. I wrote about Mom and our childhood, which was going to make him squirm when he read the blog. And he's going to read it only to make sure I didn't write about Barney. That's what he gets for trying to dictate what I write about.

When I needed to escape from inside these walls, I imagined I was a whale and these walls contained all the world's oceans. Then every shore, near and far, was within my reach.

It was Nigel's idea to go grocery shopping at midnight because, usually, there were only a handful of shoppers in the store at that time of night. He was wrong. There wasn't even a handful. The store was empty except for the two of us, two cashiers, and an assistant manager.

The three shelves lined with coffee in jars, cans, and bags were also empty as far as I was concerned. I wanted a large bag of Folgers Classic Roast, but the store was completely out of Folgers. Nigel picked up a bag of the store brand and put it in the cart. I took the bag out the cart and put it back on the shelf. Nigel gave me that look he gives me when he thought I was being difficult. Coffee was coffee, he said, and put two bags in the cart.

When we got to the register, Nigel realized he'd left his wallet in the car. He went to the car while the cashier rang up the groceries. The total came to $187.32, which Nigel paid with his debit card. We saved a few dollars because some of the main items on our list were on sale. Eggs were on sale. Two dozen for $1.29. A twelve-pack of Diet Coke was $2.59. And a big box of Little Debbie's oatmeal pies was $1.09.

On the way home, we made it through seven consecutive stop-lights without having to stop. It wasn't because Nigel was speeding, unless you call driving thirty in a forty-five mile-per-hour zone mashing the gas. I was about to get pissed off with Nigel's Miss-Daisy-driving-ass because I wanted to make it home before the bottom fell out the clouds. The clouds were so heavy they looked like they had pot bellies that were scuffing the ground. After all that showing off, it ended up not raining a drop.

That was three weeks ago, the last time we left this house. Three weeks. Twenty-something days. And, far too many hours for me to try to calculate.

The only thing I hated more than my fear was not knowing why I was afraid.

I felt like screaming, I was sick and tired of sitting here staring out this damn window! Instead, I held everything inside and continued staring out the window. I didn't want to turn around and look at Nigel because looking at him would piss me off. Without looking for him, it was easy to guess he was in front of the television glued to the Weather Channel with that shit-eating grin on his face. When Nigel knew he was wrong and tried to pretend everything was fine, his grin turned inward on him. He sat there, pretending our world was perfect when I was a few seconds away from rearranging his front teeth. It was a good thing he didn't say anything to me—anything—or even look at me wrong because I was ready to bust him in the mouth.

Nigel signed seven of the eight cover letters I left on the desk for him. I had a feeling he wasn't going to sign the letter to Aman Realty. I included the resume and letter to Richard Aman to see if Nigel would prove me wrong for once. But as usual, he didn't.

The hard part was mailing them. We had a new carrier. Friday was the last day for Vernon, our last carrier, and he didn't know who was going to replace him on this route until Friday. That's when he told me that a young black guy name Billy would replace him. Billy worked this route for three days last summer while Vernon was out on medical leave. I didn't meet him then because we didn't have any mail those three days, so I had not had a chance to explain our mail delivery routine: I'd retreat to the bedroom, Vernon would open the door, bring the mail inside, and pick up any out-going mail. After he closed the door and left, I would come out. Friday, Vernon said he would explain the delivery system to Billy. I was glad he did.

Nigel was still in bed; probably on purpose. So, I had to give the seven envelopes to the mail carrier when he came by. Vernon used to come by around ten-thirty. Since it was drizzling outside and Billy wasn't as used to the route as Vernon was, I figured he'd be a little late. I started to wake Nigel and let him give Billy the letters, but I didn't want to bother him. It took a Herculean effort for him to sign the cover letters.

Our mailbox was on the wall to the right of the front door. It's too small to put the envelopes inside, but even if it wasn't, I still would have to open the door which would be a problem. I sat by the window and waited for Billy, who would stop at Professor Childers' curbside mailbox before stopping here.

What if there's no mail for us today? my conscience reminded me.

I hadn't thought about that. If there was no mail, Billy wouldn't have to stop. I saw the mail truck pull up to Professor Childers' mailbox and stop. I thought about waking Nigel as I watched Billy put two envelopes in the mailbox. He pulled away slowly, moving closer to our house.

"Please stop here," I pleaded, my face pressed against the window. "Please stop. Please."

The mail truck turned in our driveway.

"Thank you."

Billy saw me in the window and waved as he got out the truck. I held up the manila envelopes so he could see them. Billy acknowledged with a nod and walked toward the front door. I inhaled and held my breath as I walked over to the door. Unlocking the door wasn't that hard, but turning the doorknob was a colossal task. Billy knocked on the door. I tried to turn the knob, but I couldn't. I tried again and the knob turned. The seal broke and the world poured in through a crack too thin for light to pass through.

I was freezing, drowning, dying. I fell against the door, slamming it shut.

"Are you all right?" Billy asked from the other side of the door. He waited for an answer, but my lips were frozen stiff. "Tell you what," he said. "Let's do this the way Vernon did it."

I couldn't answer. I was thawing. Shivering. Breathing air again.

"Did you hear me?" Billy asked.

"The table by the door," I responded and placed the envelopes on the table. I hurried to my bedroom and slammed the door behind me.

I heard Billy yell, "I'm coming in." A few seconds later, he yelled as he left, "I'm closing the door behind me. See you tomorrow." I heard the front door close.

Professor Anthony Childers, a chain-smoking, nonconforming Brit, taught international relations at Florida State University. Sometimes, mostly when he's a little tipsy and longing to hear a voice other than his own, he stopped Nigel in the driveway to chat about news and politics. Nigel would stand there and listen, steadily nodding in agreement, and listen some more. After thirty minutes or so, I'd tap on the window and beckon for Nigel or pretend he had an important call by waving the phone in the air. Professor Childers and Nigel hadn't hung out in over a month. I guess that's why the professor spent the afternoon standing in his driveway waving at motorists speeding by on Circle Drive.

I'm surrounded by boundless and untouchable shores that arose outside the windows, doors, and walls of 207 Circle Drive.

I hated not being able to share the few memories that I did have with Nigel, especially the ones of Mom and Dad. He's already told me the reason he won't acknowledge reading my blog. Although the blogs were about conjectured memories, they were still mostly about Mom and Dad. What I recalled about Mom and Dad weren't real memories, but I felt deep down that they couldn't all be things I made up. Sometimes, what I remembered was a smile, laughter, or a touch. And sometimes, it's the feeling there was really a Mom and Dad and not hazy images of the faces in the portraits hanging on our walls. If I could really share my thoughts with Nigel, he could fill in the blanks. I didn't know why Nigel hid from his memories of Mom and Dad. The last time I heard him mention

Mom or Dad was eleven years ago when he told me I was alive and they were dead. He never said how they died, and I never asked. I still didn't know what happened to Mom and Dad or to me because I was too afraid to ask.

A long time ago, before this life, before I evolved, I left footprints in the sands of the world outside.

My brother was essential to my existence. Without him, and without memories of my own, who would I be? Who? Nigel gave me a past and a future. His life was my life. He and I were...me.

We are each other's barber. One day, while Nigel was giving me an edge, he asked me if I dreamed when I was asleep, and if so, was I inside this house in my dreams. I didn't know what made him ask, but his tone begged for confirmation. So I told him, "Of course, I dream. Doesn't everybody? And no, I'm not hanging out inside this house." Then I pointed out the window. "I'm out there." I think it gave Nigel solace with the knowledge that I get to live a life outside these walls even if it's only in my dreams. I loved my brother too much to tell him the truth. Fear dwelled inside my dreams. I hated my fear.

I knew why whales beached themselves. They were irresistibly drawn to the shore by inborn memories and abetting dreams of whales that once trudged across dry land.

AUTUMN

CHAPTER 7

She was his first. And she was there when time stopped.

Nigel wasn't sure of the duration, but he was certain time stopped the night he spent with her. He felt the earth when it wobbled and ceased spinning. He watched as the past, present, and future embraced each other with overt skepticism. No one would believe him if he tried to explain how time stood still, so he never told anyone about the night he drank too many Kamikazes during a homecoming weekend party at his fraternity house and bedded a beautiful woman who drank almost as many. There were large chunks missing from his recollection of that night. He remembered dancing on the frat house lawn and bumping into her as she gyrated to the infectious beat of songstress Billie Lawrence's "Happiness." But he didn't remember reaching for her hand, then following her up the stairs. He recalled pointing to his room and her opening the door, but he didn't remember her unbuckling his belt, taking off his pants, or the awe-struck look on his face when he saw her naked. The moment he gave himself to her was unforgettable. Even now, fourteen years later, he still shuddered when the unsolicited memory of that night forced him to feel the dizzying sensation of sempiternity he felt inside her. He remembered very little after that moment, and he never tried to fill in the blanks. The only thing he carried with him from that night was an absolute certainty that it was possible to stop time.

Nigel was in his third year at Howard University the night time staggered. He joined the Chi Alpha fraternity and moved into the frat house during his sophomore year. Nigel was twenty-one and still a virgin. Until that night, he managed to avoid the smorgasbord of sexual entrees dropped in his lap during the salacious house parties by telling his brothers he was in love with and faithful to his high school sweetheart. Some of the brothers became doubtful about this girlfriend at home who never called and whom he never called, but none pressed the issue.

Two of Nigel's frat brothers saw her tiptoe out of his bedroom half-dressed early the next morning. They tried to peep inside at Nigel, but she closed the door before they could, which, as it turned out, was a good thing. If they had seen Nigel, the bewildered look of a drowning man just below the water's whitecaps would become part of their own catalog of unbidden memories.

They teased Nigel during lunch, but Nigel told them nothing happened between him and the girl. He said they sat up and talked the entire night. The brothers were nearly convinced until one of them asked, "What's her name?"

And Nigel answered truthfully, "I didn't ask."

He spent the rest of the day and the next few weeks wondering why he didn't ask her name or why didn't she tell him. The questions piled up. Why didn't either one of them say a word the next morning before she got dressed and rushed out the door? Did he say or do something he shouldn't have that night? Was he...you know... okay? He knew size wasn't the problem because he was more than endowed. But, was he doing it right? Did she sense that it was his first time? Was she startled? Frightened? Amazed when time stopped?

Nigel saw her three times after that night. The first time was two weeks later in the campus bookstore. He was at the register buying a copy of *The Associated Press Stylebook* when she walked in. Their eyes met briefly but neither made an attempt at acknowledgment. She walked by the register—close enough to touch him—and continued to the back of the store. Nigel paid for his handbook and walked out of the store. The next time he saw her, he was leaving campus for a weekend trip home. He was waiting at a stoplight when she walked across the street. She turned and glanced at him as she passed in front of his Corolla. Once again, their eyes met before Nigel drove off and she disappeared in the mass of students scrambling to class. It was a year later, when their paths crossed again. He was on campus transferring his records to Richmond University, which was only twelve miles from the hospital where Caleb lay in a coma. After leaving the registrar's office, Nigel stopped by the frat house to see his Chi Alpha brothers. One of the brothers was introducing him to the fraternity's new pledges when he saw her playing pool in the den with two other young women. That time, he pretended not to see her, and she returned the favor. After that day, she became another indiscernible face in a graveyard of people he once knew.

It had been twelve years since he'd last seen her, but at four o'clock this morning, she opened the door without knocking, walked in, kicked off her glass-heel slingbacks, crawled over Nigel to get to her side of the bed, then snatched the pillow from under his head and started hogging the covers. She wasn't an unexpected or unwelcome guest though. She was there because Nigel summoned her. Later that morning, on the second Monday in October, Nigel would begin a new life as an assistant professor of journalism and he was terrified. He was not ready to start living again. He needed more time. Or—which he considered more probable—for time to desist and suspend itself again.

She was here—inside 207 Circle Drive—because she was there the night time stopped in its tracks. She was his first.

CHAPTER 8 ✦ NIGEL

listen to my story. Then listen to Caleb's story. It will not be the same old story of two brothers sharing one life, because this time the plot will change as we live it. And how this telling ends is not entirely up to me.

This is our story.

This will be our life.

For almost everyone I knew, starting a new job was an uplifting experience, but for me, it was a tense, unsettling time. Having to learn and perform new and different tasks wasn't part of my dilemma. I was a fast learner and I was confident in my skills and ability. The real problem with my new job was all the new characters, different settings, and unforeseen plot twists that would be brought into our story. Everything about our life was about to change. Everything. Except for the way we lived it.

I earned my bachelor's degree in journalism and my master's degree in mass communication from Richmond University within a year of Caleb coming home from the hospital. By then, we were already settled into an amnesic existence where nothing mattered but the moment we were living in. There was no past hanging over our shoulders like leaded duffle bags. No leash around our necks for time to wrench us toward a dubious future. We were reborn each day. I attended class and when I came home, I shared my day with Caleb. We studied together and we took turns completing class assignments. Caleb was happy with our life and I wanted things to stay that way. So I decided to stay in college and work toward a doctor of philosophy degree. Eighteen months later, I earned my Ph.D. in mass communication. That's when Caleb persuaded me to get my first job. He liked our lives as students, but he wanted more. He said he was ready for us to grow up.

"We can't get stuck here," he said. "It's time for us to move on. There is a huge world out there, and we have to find our place in it."

A few weeks later, I was hired as a features writer for the *Capitol Sentinel.* Then we packed the ashen remnants of our world into a U-Haul and relocated to Tallahassee. There, our life started over.

Our new job meant starting over again. We both knew this. We weren't moving anywhere, but everything else about our life was going to change. The route we took to work. The people we worked with. The students we taught. The work we did. Our entire day; it was all about to change. Neither one of us expected the change to come easy because it didn't when we moved here.

"Butterflies?"

"Yeah, butterflies. You may not have been nervous, but I was nervous as hell about teaching our first class. And having to wait in the dark didn't help any."

"Why was it dark?"

"We couldn't find the main light switch, so the only light in the lecture hall was the small light on the podium."

"How many students does the lecture hall seat?"

"I'd guess about two-hundred."

"So, it's about the size of Leigh Hall at Richmond?"

"Yeah. Yeah. SJC's lecture hall even looks a little bit like Leigh Hall."

Caleb stared at the ceiling as I described what little I could see in the lecture hall and the anxiety I felt waiting for our first class of students to enter. His eyes were doused by a shimmering light that infused him into the picture I'd sketched for him. As I recounted waiting on students, in his mind, he was standing beside me at the podium inside SJC's lecture hall. We were both counting down the minutes. I was a nervous wreck. The smile on Caleb's face made finding the light switch totally unnecessary.

"Then...?"

"The double doors at the back opened and four students walked in. I told them it was dark because I couldn't find the light switch. One of the students walked down an exterior aisle to the front of the lecture hall and turned the lights on."

"A girl or guy?"

"A guy. Kind of short. Dark complexion and long, nappy dreads. He sat in the middle of the second row with the three guys he came in with. One of the guys was white. He had that cool hipster look, so he fit right in. Didn't seem a bit out of place."

"So the Hill is fairly integrated?"

"I wouldn't say integrated, but I saw quite a few white students on campus."

"Good," Caleb said. "I like hearing that."

"Writing For Mass Communication is the name of the course we'll be teaching. It's an introductory writing class for sophomores and juniors pursuing degrees in journalism, public relations, or advertising. There are two classes with a combined total of 136 students—seventy-seven are registered for first period and fifty-nine for third period. Both classes meet on Mondays, Wednesdays, and Fridays."

"I'll bet half of the students didn't show up today."

"Pay up. All but seven were there. A couple of the students said they received an email stating that everybody enrolled in the course would get an *A* for showing up today because the college couldn't find a replacement for Professor Kapral, who took a medical leave to begin chemotherapy five weeks after the semester started."

Caleb reluctantly asked, "What type cancer...?"

"Lung cancer. I had a brief meeting with him right before class. He doesn't look sick, but I'm guessing it's because the cancer was discovered at an early stage. He looks to be in his early fifties. Short. Stocky, with way too curly hair."

Caleb looked out the window. He wasn't showing up for the meeting with Professor Kapral.

I brought him back into our day by telling him, "Our office is on the third floor of the School of Journalism. It's a little cramped and there isn't much we can do to liven it up, except for hanging a few pictures on the wall."

Caleb stared at the ceiling again. "A plant or two will help," he suggested. "Artificial of course. A couple of large plants will set it off."

"That might work," I responded.

We spent the next hour sharing my day, eating dinner at seven o'clock while watching *Wheel of Fortune* and *Jeopardy* on TV. Caleb finished the dishes before he walked into the living room, sat in Dad's recliner, and watched as I skipped from channel to channel.

This was the story of our life. The plot, setting, and supporting characters were different, but the story read the same.

Finally. A hurricane—Florida's only hit this year—made land close enough to Tallahassee to send locals scrambling for safer ground and shelter. Professor Childers packed a few belongings in his vintage yellow Volkswagen and skirted off yesterday. It was only a category two but that was good enough for me. The hurricane's outer bands spanked Tallahassee for an entire day. Caleb hated bad weather so he turned his bedroom into a bunker, which meant I got to ride out the storm in Dad's recliner.

Caleb and I were not alone today because hurricanes incarcerated thousands, even millions of people inside solitary havens like ours. Today, we were all evacuees of the inhospitable world outside our doors.

Florida Agricultural & Mechanical University, a historically black university, sat atop one of the highest hills in Tallahassee, so the locals referred to the campus as "the Hill."

I started walking by "the Set" on my way to and from lunch twice a week. I could take another less traveled route, but I didn't. The set was the main hangout spot on the Hill. Students congregated outside on the plaza between classes, and it's often the stage for fraternity and sorority step shows, as well as social and political rallies. Dr. Hubert Alexander, who heads the journalism department, talked me into walking over to the Set during lunch to watch the homecoming week step show featuring the Kappa, Sigma, Omega, and Chi Alpha fraternities. While waiting for the show to get started, Dr. Alexander told me he pledged Kappa at FAMU twenty-seven years ago and the thing he missed most about his college days was stepping with his brothers. I saw the longing in his eyes when the Kappas kicked things off with a sharp chanting step with their red and white walking canes. Changing the pace, they wooed the crowd with a slightly erotic, yet chivalric, routine to "Gigolos Get Lonely Too" by the popular '80s band, Morris Day and The Time. The Sigmas followed with an explosive display of hip-hop choreography and precision timing. Then the Chi Alphas took to the stage and artfully recreated the frat's signature step and chant. I knew their routine step for step, word for word, as the memories of the exact routine with my brothers at Howard rushed to the forefront. I tried my best to ignore the chanting in my head, but the words and the rhythm kept flowing. My feet wanted to move, to step and tap, to stomp, but I would not give them permission. Evidently, they didn't need it because they stomped anyway. Normally, I don't let myself miss or even think about my foregone existence, but since I had no other choice, I gave in. Unguarded. And guiltless. Ravenously, I reminisced.

The girl whose name I never knew showed up again. That's why I didn't look back. I was musing about my days at Howard. My first two years living in the dorm. Pledging Chi Alpha. Stepping with my brothers. Dad helping me move into the fraternity house he helped construct when he was a student at Howard. I wasn't thinking about her or that drunken night at the frat house, so her showing up was unexpected.

I started to hate her for showing up like this. Damn started to. I hated her.

The first time a guy had sex was a pivotal moment in his life. It's a tale he would tell and retell until he's reborn into eternity. She was my first and she left too many holes in my story. If I wanted to tell someone and tell it like I remembered it, the discontinuity would make the plot impossible to follow, so I never told anyone about my first time. It wasn't entirely her fault, but I needed to blame somebody. Why not blame her? I wanted my first time to be with a woman I cared about or at least a woman whose name I knew.

If I told myself the truth, I could've gotten over not knowing her name by caulking the holes in my story. But I couldn't forgive her for looking me in the eyes three times after that night and walking away without saying a word. The last time I saw her, she looked through me like I wasn't even there. That was the real reason I hated her.

I wondered if my fascination with the woman I met at Barney's funeral had something to do with me and the girl from Howard. She was the first woman I made love to and I never knew her name. Now, I was falling helplessly in love with another woman whose name I didn't know. I didn't know if she even lived in Tallahassee, but whenever I left the house, I find myself combing the city hoping to see her. My hypothesis was, since she was at Barney's funeral, she's involved in government. I changed my route to work. Now, I took the parkway to Monroe Street, which passed directly through the government district. I could hardly keep my eyes on the road driving to and from campus. At the supermarket, I wandered down more aisles looking for her than I did for the items on Caleb's grocery list. And as much as I hated malls, I'd spent a few Saturday afternoons roaming around the Governor's Square Mall, the Tallahassee Mall, and nearly every shopping center in town hoping to see her. I couldn't stop hoping, and I didn't think I wanted to.

I was a virgin until I was twenty-one. I was saving myself for the woman I would marry one day…whoever she turned out to be. On my fifteenth birthday, during his birds and bees lecture, Dad told me that Mom was the first woman he had sex with and it was on their wedding night. He also said, and proud of the fact, that Mom was the only woman he had ever been intimate with. From that moment on, I wanted the kind of love and marriage my parents had. I wanted my future wife to be my first and my last lover. Unfortunately, that's not the way it happened. My first time was with a girl whose name I didn't know. I had sex a few more times with two other women, both casual acquaintances at Howard, but those escapades were sex, nothing more. That was a long, long time ago.

Caleb was still a virgin, as far as I was aware. Unless he got it on with one of the neighborhood girls before that December night thirteen years ago, he's a virgin. Sometimes, I wonder if he even thought about women and sex. He never talked about it, but then there are a lot of things we didn't talk about.

Barney Aman was someone we didn't talk about anymore. I caught myself thinking about Barney quite often, but I never talked about him with Caleb. I've even driven twelve miles across town more than once or twice to ride by Barney's unoccupied house, which Richard Aman refused to sell, rent, or set foot in after his son's death. Barney's ordeal changed me, and I was not sure whether it's for the better or worse. My current job was the most obvious change, but I'd changed in ways no one could see. Now, my heart beat with unbridled rhapsody after finding a reason to live at a cemetery. When I saw Frances at Barney's burial, I remembered why Barney said he stayed in the relationship with a married woman and a dangerous secret for so long.

"I loved her," Barney admitted to me the evening I stopped by his house with the manila envelope. "Frances and I had been seeing each other for years before her husband found out."

"Why is Frances suggesting you had something to do with his death?" I asked.

"Well, I don't remember much about that night because I'd been drinking. But, Frances and I were at a motel when he burst in. They argued but ended up leaving together. I guess I passed out afterwards. But, I woke up the next morning in another motel room fifty miles away with blood stains on my clothes. And I don't remember how I got there. So, I don't know what part I played in Terry's death."

"Did you and Frances ever talk about it?"

"No. We never spoke a word about that night."

Then he told me, "She thought we would be able to come out publicly with our relationship, but after that night, I began to withdraw from her."

I assured Barney his secret was safe with me. Still, it was obvious the exposure made him uneasy, including my part in covering it up. In hindsight, it was at that moment when Barney began searching for a way out.

As I opened the front door to leave, Barney asked in a forlorn tone, "Nigel, have you ever really loved someone?"

My illusory smile answered for me.

Despite its tragic ending, Barney's ordeal affected me more than I realized. I was content with the emptiness of my life until the day that manila envelope landed on my desk. After Barney's death, I began to consider the possibility of having more in my life; of simply having a life. I wanted to live; to love and be loved. Then I saw her at the cemetery. I may never see her again, but it felt good to know that my heart, though freezer burnt, was still capable of feeling love and desire.

It was the Wednesday before our two-day Thanksgiving break. I was at a university-sponsored faculty luncheon when she walked in the Grand Ballroom and sat at a table near the door. Until that moment, it never occurred to me to associate the orange and green Rattler umbrella she carried at the cemetery with FAMU's school colors and mascot. I thought I was dreaming, so I felt for the tape on my eyes. I was awake which meant she was real. After five months, I couldn't believe I was actually looking at her.

I was sitting at a table across the ballroom from where she was seated. Dr. Alexander and Dr. Phyllis Sneeds, a journalism ethics professor, were sitting at the table with me. They talked constantly as we dined on a catered lunch of steaks, baked potato, greens salad, and chocolate cake. Their back-and-forth banner during the president's address didn't bother me, because I couldn't hear them or the speech. I was too busy taking her in. I knew I wasn't going to mention her when I gave Caleb the details of our day, but I still asked myself all the questions he would ask if I did include her.

How does she look?

She's a Halle.

Monster's Ball *Halle or* Jinx *Halle?*

Jinx.

Her eyes?

Alluring. Soft brown.

Hair?

Mid-length. Silky straight. Dark with subtle highlights.

What was she wearing?

A beige, fitted turtleneck sweater and a brown skirt that hung half-way over her knee-high tan boots.

Who was she sitting with?

Two nice-looking, middle-age women. I assumed they're professors since it was a faculty luncheon.

What does she teach?

I don't know, but if I had to guess, I would probably say she teaches something in political science or business.

Then, for some unknown reason, I would blurt out, Caleb, man you should see her smile!

He'd clear his throat, take his time sitting up in Dad's recliner, and ask nonchalantly, Her smile?

Yeah, her smile. It's really something to behold.

Finally, he would ask the question that plagued me the entire luncheon. What's her name?

Her name?

Yeah. Her name.

Damn. That's strange. I'm coming up blank. What is her name?

You're so full of shit. You didn't ask her.

I was going to, but after the luncheon, she was busy mingling with some of the other professors. I guessed she already knew them. When they were done talking, she walked across campus to the School of Business faculty parking lot and got in her silver Pathfinder and drove off before I could ask her.

And then...?

Then I walked back across campus to where I was parked, got in my car, and drove home.

CHAPTER 9

It was a Monday morning three years ago.

Life went on as usual outside.

There was no mail so Vernon, the mailman, looked toward the front window and waved as he drove by.

Across the street, joggers and most of the hikers zipped by Mr. and Mrs. Retired Walker, who held hands as they took their daily stroll on the meandering trails at Myers Park. Caleb and Nigel moved into the red brick house on Circle Drive six years ago, and since then, Caleb has watched the couple grow older and walk closer to each other. He didn't know their names, but after several weeks of seeing them almost daily, Caleb christened the couple Mr. and Mrs. Retired Walker.

A much younger couple, both doctoral students at Florida State University and new residents of the Myers Park neighborhood, played a frisky game of twenty-one on the basketball court. On the tennis courts, two bureaucratic housewives played their weekly game of tennis while their nannies tended to the toddlers on the playground. And a park worker sang to himself as he circled the baseball field aboard one of the maintenance department's new riding mowers.

Several blocks from Myers Park, the trading floors opened in downtown Tallahassee as lobbyists and lawmakers began doing business over brunch and Cuban cigars during their mid-morning session break.

A few blocks farther north, in the *Sentinel*'s newsroom, Nigel conducted a phone interview with the Springtime Tallahassee Parade coordinator.

Life went on as usual outside 207 Circle Drive. But inside—behind its suppressive doors, windows, and walls—Caleb was realizing a frightening truth: Death was the absence of a life and not the end of all life.

Two seconds earlier, Caleb stepped off the armrest of his dad's black recliner. A minute before that, he took his shoes off, stood on the recliner, and tied the loose end of a twisted bed sheet around his neck. Thirty seconds before that he dragged the recliner from its post by the window to the middle of the floor. It took twenty-two minutes to disconnect the ceiling fan from the beam, then attach the sheet to the beam. About a minute and a half to compose a note to Nigel stating, *I love you Nigel. Live.* And six minutes to build up the courage to go through with the decision he'd contemplated for nearly two months. So it had been nearly a half hour since Caleb decided he could no longer live inside a coffin.

It was two hours before noon.

Caleb did not die a physical death that morning, but he finally lay to rest the hope that he would one day disremember the malignant taste of fear. Ironically, it was his fear that saved him that morning. Two seconds after stepping off the armrest, when he saw his life flash before him, a grotesquely rendered picture emerged of an eternity spent outside these walls. Of never-ending freezing and breathing water. Of an end to his story. Of the look on Nigel's face when he opened the front door. Of Nigel alone. Until that moment, Caleb saw death as his way out—his ticket to a life without fear. But trying to die showed him that death was merely a conclusion and the only thing afterward was a future without him...at least in this world. He would cease to exist, but life and time would not. So he decided to keep living. He grabbed the noose and fought desperately to get his legs around the backrest of the recliner. The noose, anticipating his change of mind, tightened around his neck. His lungs were about to implode. He used his legs to pull himself on top of the backrest and loosen the tension on the bedspread. He fell off the recliner during his rush to untie the noose. Then he struggled to fill his deprived lungs. He clung to the floor for nearly a minute, trying to erase the picture inside his head. It took fifteen seconds to push the recliner back over by the window. Forty minutes to untie the sheet and reattach the ceiling fan to the beam. Thirty-two seconds to burn his note to Nigel in the kitchen sink. Less than a second to resolve that Nigel never needed to know about the hanging man. Another five minutes to put the navy blue and white sheet back on his bed, then make the bed. And the rest of his life to live with the morning, he tried to exorcise his fear.

It was still an hour before noon.

Caleb spent the rest of the afternoon sitting in his dad's black recliner staring out the window. He wasn't sure whether he or the world outside had changed but something was different. Everything looked the same. People frolicked about at the park. Cars barely missed each other as they jostled on Circle Drive. Professor Childers, wearing a gray tweed jacket and matching cap, waved at passing motorists as he strolled to his mailbox. The world out there was still the same. Caleb held his hand in front of his face. The burrowed lifelines in his palms were still shaped like a *W.* Both hands still had the small nubs of sixth fingers that were cut off at birth. He pressed his hands against the window and realized how fear can exaggerate—turn inches into miles. The distance between his hands and the other side of the window had become immeasurable.

Caleb decided right then to forget everything that transpired that morning. He felt he was entitled to purposefully erase this attempt at dying since God fixed it so he didn't have to remember his first death. He began to tell himself all the things he would no longer remember. As he selectively uttered the words aloud, one behind the other, the words disseminated into syllables, letters, sounds, thoughts, then into nothingness.

"...was tired."

"The ceiling..."

" ...tied..."

"B-r-e-a-t-h-i-n-g..."

"...D-e..."

" "

He forgot the ineffable agony of a constricting noose around the neck of a hanging man. Then he released the anger that he deemed tangible, flowing as fluidly as blood. Caleb made the choice to be happy living in his world with its sequestered walls and telescopic windows; its flinty hardwood floors and crumbling sky; and the canned meadows and mountains and oceans that colored its vapid air. He didn't fool himself into believing everything he hated about his world had suddenly become appealing. Instead, he gratefully accepted his friable life for what it was, because now he knew that ending the story was way harder than living it.

M y world was unchanging. I could paint these walls every color in the heavens, but I would still be living within a dungeon of reachable moons and planets and stars inside galaxies that go on and on forever.

Our life was turning Nigel into an old man way before his time. And as much as I hated to take the blame for it, my condition had a lot to do with his premature aging. Don't get me wrong, he didn't look bad for his age. What's breaking down was Nigel's spirit. He had the spirit of a man who knew he'd lived too long and the only thing he had to look forward to was the rare night his dreams transported him back to one of the few happy moments of his prior life. Something akin to catching a Hail Mary pass and scoring a touchdown during the last seconds of the game to win the district championship for his high school football team, or seeing the smile on our mother's face at the surprise party we gave her on her forty-third birthday, or fishing in Flatley Creek with Dad and me. Nigel had a long life ahead of him, but he acted like all his happy moments have already been lived and captured in the framed portraits lining our hallway and living room walls.

I hoped this new job as an assistant professor of journalism at FAMU would lift his spirits. I sent out seven resumes and, within a week, Nigel received five calls for interviews. The call I was hoping for came first. Nigel was sitting by the phone when Dr. Hubert Alexander, FAMU's journalism department chairperson, called but he didn't budge. I answered the phone and pretended I was Nigel. Dr. Alexander said he admired our work for the *Capitol Sentinel* and he was extremely interested in meeting with us to discuss the assistant professor position. I, well me as Nigel, told Dr. Alexander I could meet with him the next day. He asked if ten-thirty would be a good time, and I told him ten-thirty was fine. When I hung up the phone, Nigel, who was playing tic-tac-toe with the TV remote, asked who I was talking to. I answered him with a question, "What did you say, Professor Greene?"

"So I've got an interview at FAMU tomorrow?"

"The interview is only a formality. Trust me. You've already got the job."

"We'll see," Nigel responded in his drabbest tone.

I wasn't about to let Nigel spoil my excitement, so I pretended not to hear his cynicism. Besides, I had to get him ready for the interview—make sure he looked the part.

His bedroom was dark even with the light on, so I opened the curtains and blinds. The sunlight poured in. That's when I noticed the wastebasket next to the nightstand. It was filled with wads of used paper tape. A nearly empty roll of tape was on the nightstand. Paper tape is Nigel's constant bedmate. A few years ago, when Nigel was cuddling with regular Scotch tape, he went around for months without any eyebrows or lashes. I never said anything to him about it, but from the despairing expression on his face, it had been a long time since sleep delivered a pleasant dream. I was not blind, regardless of what Nigel might believe, that I don't see the incessant hurt he lives with, but I see everything. I simply pretend not to. I had to pretend for his sake and for my own. To see Nigel's life—our life—for what it really was would mean having to ask myself what had happened to make me so fearful of the world outside our door.

I turned the light on in Nigel's closet and walked inside. Everything was in place. The twelve shoe boxes were stacked neatly against the wall. On the front of each box was a Polaroid of the shoes inside. Putting a Polaroid on the outside of each box was an organizing tip I picked up from a guest on *Oprah*. Nigel's dress and work clothes took up one side of the closet. Seven hangers on the other side of the closet held his casual clothes, a few pairs of jeans and khakis with button-up shirts to match. Everything in the closet was black, gray, navy, khaki, or blue jeans. I selected a two-piece gray suit that I ordered a few months ago from Dillard's for Nigel to wear to a local media awards banquet. The suit would be okay for the interview with Dr. Alexander, but I knew I was going to have to revamp my brother's look before he started his new job. I couldn't have him on the Hill looking shabby.

I picked up the cordless phone and walked to my bedroom as soon as I saw Nigel get out of the car. It was ten minutes after two. The interview was at 10:30. FAMU was a fifteen-minute drive from here, which meant Nigel left the campus about five minutes before two. I'm guessing it took him fifteen minutes to walk from the School of Journalism to his car. So at 1:40, Nigel shook hands with Dr. Alexander, thanked him, then said good-bye. The interview lasted from 10:30 until 1:40. That's over three hours. A three-hour interview and Nigel's uneasy smile let me know that it was okay to call and politely cancel the other four interviews I had scheduled for him.

I yelled from the kitchen. "Nigel, it's six-thirty and the clock's ticking. You better get a move on it."

Breakfast—hash browns, bacon, scrambled eggs, buttered toast, orange juice, and coffee—was ready, and Nigel's plate was on the kitchen counter waiting to be devoured.

"You shouldn't have gotten dressed until after you ate breakfast," I said when he walked in the kitchen. "You might get something on your clothes."

"I'm not hungry," he responded. "I'll have a glass of juice."

I gave Nigel a quick looking over. I trimmed his hair the night before so his hair was straight. He was wearing an olive-colored shirt, tie, and pants set by Sean John that I purchased online last week since I didn't have the company's catalog. I told Nigel, "You look tight."

He smiled and thanked me. Outwardly, Nigel didn't appear nervous, but the irresolute tone of his voice told the real truth: He was scared to death.

"Nigel, we can do this with our eyes closed."

He nodded, picking up a glass of juice as he walked out the kitchen. "I'm getting the newspaper," he said.

I poured a cup of coffee and went to my bedroom. I leaned against the door and listened as Nigel stepped outside into a new, uncharted world. When I heard the front door close behind him, I ran over to my bedroom window, flung the curtains open, nearly snatched the blinds down trying to wind them up, then I watched in awe as the inaugural rays of sunlight scratched and clawed their way across the primordial shag draped over 207 Circle Drive. The first day of our new life had begun.

I wanted to be a teacher when I was growing up. I couldn't remember way back then, but if I could, I'd bet you that's what I wanted to be.

Our third week as professors ended Friday with mid-term exams. We composed the exam together earlier during the week. A third of the exam—twenty multiple choice questions—focused on Associated Press guidelines and style. Another third of the exam was short answer questions. And the last part required the students to write a short news article based on an actual police report and interview notes that we provided. I'd spent most of the weekend grading the 123 exams. Last night I was up until nearly 2 a.m. I couldn't believe I enjoyed doing this as much as I did. Nigel could take it or leave. He would sit down and grade two, three, maybe even four exams, creating a reason to stop and find something else to do for a couple of hours. Today, he did our laundry, which he never did. He watched the Dolphins lose to the Patriots. After that, he watched the Titans and Broncos play a down-to-the-buzzer game that the Titans won by a field goal. He spent an hour thumbing through the four scrapbooks of articles we wrote for the *Sentinel*. He even cooked dinner. I can't remember the last time Nigel cooked anything that called for more than five minutes of microwaving, but a mouth-watering dinner—roast beef, buttered red potatoes, green beans, and yeast rolls—was served promptly at 7 o'clock.

After dinner, Nigel sat on the sofa watching *60 Minutes*. I sat in the recliner, using an end table as my desk. I'd finished the last of the exams earlier in the day, but I felt compelled to look over the short answer and writing portion of the twenty or so exams Nigel graded because he was way too heavy-handed with the red pen. Red ink dripped off of some of the exams he graded. The problem with Nigel's grading was he didn't allow for too much deviation. He expected every article to read the way he would have written it.

One of the students' articles began, "John Beatty may have gotten away with the BMW he jacked from Rachel Davis if he had not asked her to hold his jacket while he took her two-year-old son out of the car seat. He handed Davis her son and she gave Beatty his jacket. Then Beatty drove away, but without his license and the forty dollars in his wallet. He had become the victim of a pickpocket. Davis."

Nigel deducted ten points from the article and scribbled in red ink: *Were you trying to be funny? I bet Rachel Davis didn't think it was funny.*

I disagreed. I thought the opening was clever, so I added ten points back to the student's grade. I added twenty-five points to the first three exams I rechecked. Nigel watched me as I changed the grades, but it wasn't because he was concerned about the changes I made. He wanted to comment on Lesley Stahl's report about the national recall of two prescription pain drugs. I tried my best to look extremely busy since he was too polite to interrupt. It worked. Whatever he was going to tell me, he mumbled it to himself and turned his attention back to the television.

Our new life was familiar. It was reminiscent of our days at Richmond University, so all we had to do was adapt to being professors instead of grad students. I realized I needed this career change as much as Nigel. We were news reporters for the past nine years, so the majority of our life outside 207 Circle Drive was as detached observers. We were never in the story. It felt good to finally be part of what's happening. However, my excitement hadn't translated to Nigel. I wanted to be part of the world outside these walls and windows, but Nigel would still rather stay here shut away from everything.

In Tallahassee and on the Hill, people made a big deal about homecoming, so I was dying to take part in my first homecoming day. When I mentioned it to Nigel, he said he wasn't going. I insisted. Then I begged. Nigel pitched me every excuse he could come up with not to go, but I knocked them all out the park.

"I don't care that much for football," he lobbed.

That one turned into a line drive over the left field fence. "Man, stop lying! You love football. We watch football all the time."

"On TV." He tossed a curve. "I like watching it on TV."

Okay. That one went foul.

"Then don't worry about watching the game." I crowded the plate. "Let's go for the bands. We already know the Marching 100 gonna cut up."

He hurled an inside slider. "I don't want to sit in the middle of thousands of people that we don't know."

That one went over the centerfield fence and landed in a dugout on the adjacent field. "We can sit in the journalism block with Dr. Alexander and Dr. Sneeds. And, don't forget you told them we would try to make it."

We were up before 6 a.m. on Homecoming Saturday. October had been unseasonably warm so I bought Nigel an extra-large, white Hilfiger pullover shirt, a pair of tan, brown, and white plaid shorts—size 36 when he wears 34, and a pair of brown casual Campers from JCPenney. Nigel moped around like he had a hangover, but I had him dressed and out of the house by seven.

I spent the day surfing between the three local TV stations and 96.1 FM on the radio. I wanted to see and hear as much news coverage of the parade and game as I could before Nigel came home and we sat down to muse about our day.

I hoped I wasn't going to need to drag our day out of him, but it turned out Nigel had a great time and couldn't wait to relive it with me. Nigel had a better time than I did. I was dumbfounded. FAMU beat Morgan State 24-23, but the win didn't register with

Nigel. He was more enthralled by the atmosphere of the day. As I listened, I realized he unconsciously transposed pages of what I assumed was his former life into our story. Nigel described navy blue, red, and white floats and bison that were not in the parade I saw on TV. And why would they? FAMU's mascot was an orange and green rattlesnake and Morgan State's colors were orange and blue and its mascot was a bear. Nigel joked about drinking a few beers on the lawn of a frat house near Bragg Memorial Stadium before walking over to the stadium with the frat members. Nigel hanging out with frat guys? I didn't think so. Besides, there weren't any frat houses near the stadium. When he came home from work Monday, two days after homecoming, he had a diamond stud in his ear and toted a six-pack of Michelob. Two beers and twenty minutes later, he showed me a step routine that he said he saw on the Hill. He even knew the Chi Alpha chant. I didn't say anything, but I deduced the step routine and all this hanging out with frat boys had to be part of his past life because there's no way he could have learned all those steps, turns, claps, and moves after seeing the routine performed once. When he was through stepping, Nigel sat down and stared at the ceiling fan. He smiled longingly as he watched scenes from his departed life replay on the revolving blades.

It took two days for the pair of diamond earrings to arrive after I'd ordered them from Zales.com. I was sitting by the window when James Henderson, the UPS driver, pulled in the driveway. He knew the delivery routine, so I went to my bedroom and he came inside. I heard the front door close. "I'm in," he yelled.

"How's it going?" I asked, walking back in the living room.

"It's been a rough morning," Henderson replied. He gave me the package, then took a handkerchief out of his pocket and wiped the sweat off his bald head. Henderson, a former college basketball player, wasn't wearing earrings, but I noticed the pierce marks in both his earlobes. "I don't know why, but Thursdays are the worst day of the week for me."

"Well, it's only an hour until lunchtime." I signed the delivery voucher. "So, how's married life treating you?" I asked as I opened the package.

"It's been almost three months, and so far it's been smooth sailing."

"...Glad to hear that," I said and started toward the bedroom. "Peace, man." I walked in the room and closed the door. A few seconds later, I heard the front door close.

I don't think my feet touched the floor during my dash to the kitchen. I emptied a tray of ice cubes on a washcloth and wrapped the cubes inside. I put OutKast in the CD player and cranked it up. Two sewing needles were already soaking in alcohol on the shelf in the bathroom. I put the washcloth against my earlobe and waited for the numbness to set in. Five minutes later, I used one of the sewing needles to prick my earlobe. I didn't feel it, so I held my breath, then pushed the needle all the way through. It hurt too much to holler. It felt like my ear had been chopped off with a machete. Blood spilled in the sink and on the floor. After I regained my senses and pulled myself up off the floor, I put another ice cube against my earlobe and eased the needle out. I held the crimson cube on my earlobe a few more minutes to numb it before I inserted the stud. I braced myself against the sink and forced the stud through the hole. The pangs from ripping flesh drop-kicked me and I landed on the floor again. But it was done.

After cleaning the bathroom and primping in the mirror for an hour or so, I started on my afternoon chores. I did the laundry and graded the research papers Nigel brought home the day before. I cooked dinner—fried pork chops, cabbage, and macaroni and cheese. Then I sat down in Dad's recliner and counted down the minutes to Nigel's arrival. I could not wait to see the expression on his face when he saw my diamond stud.

I was in my usual spot when Nigel drove up. I waved to him and went to my bedroom. When I heard the front door open and close, I walked into the living room. Nigel was sitting on the sofa. I sat beside him so he couldn't help noticing my stud, but he pretended not to see it. So, I went ahead and asked, "How do you like my bling?"

"I saw it," he answered. That was all he said.

The next morning, Nigel walked in the kitchen while I was fixing breakfast and tossed his diamond studs in the trash. Then he poured a cup of coffee and went back to his bedroom and got dressed.

That evening, after he came home from work, Nigel put the trash bag containing two pairs of new diamond ear studs outside in the garbage.

Through these telescopic windows, I saw a world that I could only watch from a distance like the man in the moon.

The telephone rang while we were eating dinner. The phone was on the table by Nigel, but he ignored the ringing. I nearly knocked my tray over rushing to answer it. Dr. Alexander and his wife, Gloria, who we met at the homecoming game, were calling to invite us to the Fall Football Classic in Orlando between FAMU and Bethune-Cookman College. Nigel passed without even considering their offer. It would be a waste of time trying to change his mind, so I didn't bother. Besides, I was not sure I wanted to attend another football game with Nigel. I was scared he might go schizo on me again.

Florida had a new governor whose name was not Barney Aman, and I was pissed off. It's not that I disliked our new governor. He'd do a great job. I was pissed because of the miscount. My write-in vote for Barney Aman couldn't have been the only vote he received. I demanded a re-count. Forget a re-count. Barney Aman should be our new governor if for no other reason than I wanted him to be.

I hated bad weather and hurricanes were at the top of my hate list. This was my closest encounter with a hurricane. It was a category two that made land near Apalachicola Bay. I was under my bed praying our house could withstand this monstrous lashing because this was the only shelter I had. Nigel, he got a perverted kick out of weather like this, so he was having a ball. If he could, without being Baker Acted, Nigel would go outside, chain himself to one of the deep-rooted oaks, and implore, "Red Rover! Red Rover! Please send Miss Bad Ass right over."

I didn't know what it was about cold weather and traffic accidents, but when the temperature dipped, Circle Drive turned into a bumper-car rink. I understood if Tallahassee was in the North where it snowed and sometimes the roads got covered by ice, but that's not the case down here. An early morning frost wasn't uncommon, but we saw snow as often as we saw Haley's Comet. Two nights ago, a cold front drifted through and the temperature dropped into the mid-thirties. The next morning, it looked like someone had shaken a giant sifter of ice shavings over the park and neighborhood. I looked out the window while Nigel was eating breakfast and saw cars sliding on Circle Drive like they were driving on a sheet of ice. Less than ten minutes after Nigel left for work, there was a three-vehicle wreck right up the street. A red Ford Escape skidded into the back of a black Honda, causing the Honda to swerve left into the oncoming traffic, slamming into a brown sedan. I was in the kitchen cleaning up when I heard a thunderous crash. I ran into the living room, but I couldn't see the accident from the front window, so I ran into the den and opened the curtains. The view was a lot better. I could see the vehicles involved in the wreck. Professor Childers, wearing snow boots, olive-green corduroy pants, and a bulky, beige sweater and a matching wool cap, stood at the edge of his driveway, which was about forty yards from the accident. He turned and saw me at the window. He tossed a half-smoked cigarette on the ground, then lowered his head and mouthed the words, "It looks bad." I nodded, sitting on the edge of the desk. Cars were already backed up to Myers Park, and the ambulance and three police cars had a difficult time getting through to the victims. One of the officers pulled to the side of the road, got out of his car, and started directing traffic while the other two officers and the EMTs helped the victims. Professor Childers smoked six cigarettes—I counted them—as he talked with police officers and people who were closer to the accident, relaying the information to me. According to him, the man who drove the Escape was okay, but the woman and her ten-year-old daughter in the Honda and the man in the sedan sustained serious injuries. It was nearly two hours before traffic got back to normal on Circle Drive. By then, the frost had melted and the temperature had climbed to fifty-four degrees. The reality show was over. I waved goodbye to Professor Childers, closed the curtains in the den, and went to the kitchen and finished the dishes.

I spent the day writing my new blog. Since Thanksgiving was in a few days, this week's blog was titled, "The Best Meal of the Year."

"The (not so true) Way I Remember It" – by Caleb Greene

The Best Meal of the Year

When I was growing up, there were everyday kitchen rules and there were holiday kitchen rules that governed what was on the menu and how meals were prepared.

The everyday rules were open to interpretation and changed according to who was doing the cooking. However, the holiday kitchen rules were written in the stainless steel pots that were only taken off the shelf to prepare special meals.

My daddy rarely ventured in the kitchen or decided what was for dinner. However, when it came to his holiday dinner, he had one rule. Something wild better be on the menu.

My brother, Nigel, still doesn't know his way around the kitchen, but he does a great job following directions while prepping things for me.

There are no shortcuts was my mother's holiday kitchen rule. That meant when it came time to prepare what she called the best meal of the year, you cooked it from scratch. Except for pie shells, there were no frozen items. And, as I came to learn, there were no electric choppers.

When I became big enough to help out in the kitchen, I went along with their holiday kitchen rules. I still do. Well, not all of them. The one that I've broken without regret is my mother's rule about electric choppers. I don't regret it because I eventually got her to ease up on this restriction. But it wasn't easy.

We were preparing Thanksgiving dinner the first time I pulled out an electric chopper. My mother suspiciously eyed the contraption and asked, "What's that?"

"Mom, it's the electric chopper I gave you last Christmas," I answered. "I don't know why you haven't used it."

"What are you going to do with it?" she asked.

"Chop onions, celery, and green peppers," I replied and dropped an onion in the chopper to demonstrate. "All you have to do is press this button and it chops the onion for you just like that. No more tears."

She smiled approvingly and said with all the enthusiasm of watching paint dry, "Wow. It chops them up fast." Then, in the next breath, she asked, "What are you doing with those chopped onions?"

"I'm putting them in the dressing."

"No you're not," she snapped.

"Why?" I asked a little shocked by her response.

"Because I like cut onions in dressing."

"What's the difference? Cut? Chopped?"

"I like hand-cut onions in dressing," she said in the tone she used whenever she deemed a conversation over and she'd had the final say. "We'll try that electric chopper one day when we're just cooking."

A few months later, I used the electric chopper to chop onions to go in dressing for a Sunday dinner. After my mother tasted the dressing, she reconsidered her rule about electric choppers in her holiday kitchen.

The rest of the rules are still written in stainless steel.

I've come up with a Thanksgiving menu and my shopping list is complete. Now, all I have to do is shop for groceries, go hunting or beg a hunter for the menu's something wild item, then spend eight to ten hours preparing what my mother called the best meal of the year.

Something was different. I had been feeling it all day. It wasn't the food. The Thanksgiving dinner I, and my prep cook, Nigel, spent the entire morning preparing was the same as last year's and every other year that I could remember. We cooked turkey and dressing. The cornbread dressing was from Mom's recipe. Baked ham. Collard greens crammed with smoked ham hocks. Macaroni and cheese. Mom's recipe included a cup of ricotta cheese that really set it off. Potato salad was on the menu. For dessert, I baked two pumpkin pies and a five-layer coconut cake. We sat at the dining room table and ate dinner at 1:30 like we always did. As usual, Nigel devoured enough food for three people, but he said something I didn't expect. "The dressing was good, but the dressing tastes better when you chop the onions by hand," he said with a chuckle and stood, stumbled into the living room, and grabbed the remote off the table during his backward plunge on the sofa. He had read the blog.

I have a weird phobia about being alone in our dining room. Maybe it's due to the fact that it's the only time we used the dining room was for holiday dinners—occasions when families gather to reinforce the bonds that hold them together. I felt jittery, so I put my fork down without taking a bite of my second serving of turkey and dressing and followed Nigel into the living room. I stretched out in the recliner and let myself sink into the pacifying cavity Dad had left. When I looked at Nigel, I realized what was different. Nigel. He was pretending to watch television, but the flicker in his eyes divulged he was mostly somewhere else. Wherever he was, he was thrilled to be there. His unshackled smile was a rare, foreboding sight.

I didn't dwell on it at first, but Nigel had been acting kinda peculiar since he'd come home from the faculty luncheon yesterday. He'd arrived home around four, but we waited until right before dinner to discuss our day. Later that night, as I was getting ready to turn in, Nigel walked in my bedroom, sat on the edge of the bed, and started jabbering about our day again. His eyes shimmered as he gushed about the faculty luncheon like it had been a surreal and unforgettable whoop-de-do. All I could do was listen and watch as he envisioned a life that didn't include me.

I loved my brother. I really did. And I wanted him to be happy. But could you blame me for wondering what would become of our life—of my life—once Nigel found happiness in the world outside 207 Circle Drive? Well, could you?

CHAPTER 11

Every moment. Every story. Every life. Ends. But endings were only new beginnings. And, this was how their ending began.

It began when the fall semester ended nine days ago. During those nine days, Nigel began to spend more and more time with her. Every day there was something different that he had to do on campus. At least that's what he told Caleb. He was going to the office to submit final grades, to prepare for next semester, or attend faculty development workshops. But all the time, he was with her. Whenever she stopped at Lester's Gym for an early morning aerobic workout, he was parked across the street watching. They dined in the same restaurants, although not together. They went to the same theater and watched the same movie from a few rows apart. They did most of their holiday shopping at the posh shops at Meadows of Timberlake. The two of them were inseparable.

Their ending had begun and there was no turning back after the third time Nigel drove by her house on Pine Bluff Road. He slowed down; slithered by. He watched as she walked out of the house carrying a garment bag and a small suitcase. He drove three blocks to the end of the street, then turned around and made another pass.

He gazed at her as she packed three large bags filled with Christmas presents in her silver Pathfinder. She backed out of the driveway; drove down Monroe Street. Merged into eastbound traffic on Interstate 10, before veering south onto Interstate 75.

Before Nigel realized what he was doing or where he was going, he'd driven down Monroe Street. Merged into eastbound traffic on Interstate 10, veering south onto Interstate 75.

Nigel was on I-75, nearing Gainesville, when he finally looked at the gas gauge. He was riding on fumes. He hoped she would stop soon because the low-fuel light had started blinking. If he stopped for gas, he would lose her, but he didn't have a choice. He had to stop at the next exit. As he drove the three miles to the exit, he began to miss her. In a stroke of fortune that gave the impression that Heaven had heard his thoughts, her right signal flashed and the Pathfinder swerved onto the exit ramp. She pulled in the fuel plaza, then parked and went inside the store. Nigel stopped at the gas pumps. He swiped his credit card through the pay-at-the-pump scanner and filled the tank.

She bought a bottle of spring water before walking out of the store. She was getting in the Pathfinder when she glimpsed a FAMU faculty decal on the rear bumper of the black Lumina at the gas pumps. She remembered seeing the Lumina somewhere back in Tallahassee. *Probably on campus*, she thought. The driver's back was to her, so she couldn't get a good look at him. By the time she backed out and pulled over to the gas pumps, Nigel had driven away…but not too far.

He followed her onto the Florida Turnpike. He drove a short distance behind her as she cruised on Interstate 4, weaving through Orange Blossom Trail's bumper-to-bumper traffic…turned left onto Lakeshore Road…entered Summerland Village…pulled in the driveway of a small, peach and white block house on Tanner Road and parked.

She exited the Pathfinder and walked toward the house. That's when she saw the black Lumina parked on the curb right up the block. She walked out to the street and tried to get a closer look.

Nigel saw her coming his way, so he made a U-turn and sped off, but not before she saw the FAMU faculty decal on the car's rear bumper.

Summerland Village, a sprawling community of mostly first-time homeowners and retirees, was once a military family housing base, and Nigel had a hard time finding his way out of the bellicose maze of pastel-colored houses and indistinguishable lawns. An early dusk settled in by the time he found his way back to Lakeshore Road.

The drive home seemed twice as long, even though the clock and mileage gauge suggested otherwise. Nigel understood this paradox because he'd had fourteen years to acquaint himself with the various ways time operated. He knew that time didn't pass the same when you were missing from your life. Still, even though he was missing, there were questions that he couldn't evade since he was the person asking them.

Why her?

Before he could answer…

What am I doing here?

What am I going to tell Caleb?

The questions persisted.

Did I actually do this?

Or was this only a…?

What's wrong with me?

Why her?

Why her?

WINTER

CHAPTER 12 ✧ NIGEL

I allowed myself to retain only a handful of memories.

I remembered Christmas presents. The ones that could fit in boxes were wrapped in red, green or gold foil and adorned with satin bows as large as the boxes, then stacked like Legos in the guest room weeks before Thanksgiving. The Christmas tree went up on the first day of December and officially began the holiday season, but the season started months earlier for Mom. She composed and revised her Christmas shopping list throughout the month of September, and she used this list as a deterrent to bad behavior. Caleb and I would sneak into her room and search for the list that she conveniently left on the dresser. Since I was old enough to read, I'd stand in front of the mirror combing my hair, all the while glancing down at the list and calling out the items that Mom had written under our names.

"You're getting a three-speed bicycle, a remote control helicopter, and Rock 'Em Sock 'Em robots." I would have to hold Caleb down to keep him from screaming and turning cartwheels.

When I finally took my hand from over his mouth, he'd calmly ask, "What are you getting Nigel?"

"A ten-speed, a TV-tennis game, and a watch."

From September to December, a scribbled line was Mom's most dreaded method of punishment. The first misstep was met with a raised eyebrow. The sentence for the next wrong move was a dark, heavy, infectious line through an item on the list. And this was a line that couldn't be erased or even blotted out with a gallon of Liquid Paper. Caleb and I would spend the rest of the season praying and behaving and hoping the item found its way from underneath the pile of grated lead back into the locked guest room. We did everything we could to get back in Mom's favor. We washed the dishes without having to be asked. We vacuumed. We shoveled snow out of the driveway and walkway. We even shelled pecans for Mom's Christmas fruitcake, then choked down the fruitcake and pretended to like it. There was no point in wasting time or energy on Dad, thinking he might feel sorry for us and put the TV-tennis game or the Rock 'Em Sock 'Em robots on his Santa list. Mom wrote his list and did all of his shopping.

I was fourteen and Caleb was eight when Santa Claus stopped dropping down the chimney to unlock the guest room and help haul the four-story, red, gold, and green skyscraper of gifts into the living room. I was nine when I learned the Santa secret, and for five years, Mom forced me to keep it from Caleb. Finally, when I was twelve, she let me stay up and help. I enjoyed two years of pretending to make my own Santa list, which I used to manipulate Caleb. The year Caleb connected the dots and put it all together was the year Christmas took on an entirely different meaning for our family. The holiday season was no longer about presents, a jolly old man in a red and white suit, and lights and songs. This special time of year, Mom explained, was really about God's greatest gift to mankind: His son, His love, and His forgiveness.

Except for the small fire in the fireplace, there were no visible changes in the way we celebrated the season. The living room, the den, the hallways, the dining room, and the yard were all elegantly trimmed in strings of glistening clear lights and green garland and oversized red bows decorated with gold and green trinkets and holly and glazed pinecones. Mom still started her shopping list the first week of September, and she still used the dreaded line to regulate us. In early October, the door of the guest room was closed and locked until Christmas morning. Mom continued her traditions of piping Christmas music throughout the house during dinner and surprising Caleb, Dad, and me with small pre-Christmas gifts during the weeks leading up to the big reveal. The only thing missing was the magic.

I yearned for the Christmas of my youth. I wished I could see the world the way I saw it when I was a six-year-old who still believed in Santa Claus. I'd gladly trade a year of my life to see the world for five minutes through the eyes of that six-year-old who didn't consider the irrationality of a three-hundred-pound elderly man crawling up and down the chimney of nearly every house in the world within the span of one night. There was no enchantment in the world after Santa disappeared from Christmas. The Easter Bunny. Witches and goblins. Tooth fairies. The Sandman. Happy-ever-after stories. Wishes coming true. They all became man-made concoctions to help make life more than a coming and going. Magic and miracles ceased to exist. What I really wanted for Christmas was to close my eyes, open them and believe again.

Our holiday season was a prolonged series of dated rituals. For the past few years, I'd basically gone through the motions and let Caleb handle everything. This year, Caleb had been acting like a scrooge, so I had to take the helm. The first day of December was the day we put up the Christmas tree, like Mom did. Normally, on the day after Thanksgiving, Caleb pulled all the Christmas decorations out the closets and tested every string of lights. This year, he sat around like the day after Thanksgiving was like any old day. I asked him if something was wrong and he shrugged his shoulders and said no. I didn't believe him, but I didn't press the issue. I figured he'd take the decoration and lights out the next day, but he didn't.

The morning of the first, before I went to work and after we ate breakfast, I told Caleb I was going outside to get the newspaper. When he walked in his room and closed the door, I opened the front door and left it open while I hurriedly pulled the storage boxes out the closets.

"Nigel," Caleb shouted from his room. "What are you doing?" I didn't answer.

Caleb yelled, "I thought you were going to get the paper!"

I went outside and got the newspaper from the delivery box. I put the newspaper on the sofa, grabbed my briefcase and keys, hurried out the door, and slammed it behind me. I ran to the car because Caleb would be standing at the front window cursing and screaming as soon as he heard the front door close. And he was. I pretended not to hear or see him as I backed out of the driveway.

It was the week before finals, which meant there were no classes, so I left work early and stopped by a tree lot in front of Publix. The lot attendant, a young man with a spiked goatee and a tattooed chain around his neck, told me to browse and let him know when I found a tree I liked. I chose the second tree I saw.

Caleb wasn't standing at the front window when I pulled in the driveway, but I noticed Dad's recliner had been moved to the side window. I untied the tree and took it off the roof of the car. When I opened the front door, I saw strings of lights and other decoration covering the living room floor. When Caleb heard the front door close, he walked out of his bedroom and into the living room. I dropped my briefcase and keys on the floor, putting the tree down by the front window. I turned and smiled at Caleb as he sat in Dad's recliner. "We had a pretty good day today," I began.

"I'm sure we did," Caleb responded dryly.

"What's with the attitude?"

Caleb glanced around the living room. "Who are you talking to?"

"Don't worry about it. We can do this later." I picked up my briefcase and walked toward my bedroom. "Let me know when you're up to it." I closed the door and spent the rest of the evening in my room working on the semester's final exam. When I emerged from my bedroom after midnight, the tree was decorated and the living room, the den, and hallways were trimmed in pine garland and red, white, and green candles, and frosted pinecones, and an assortment of red bows. A box labeled "Outside Lights" was by the front door.

There were no classes during finals week, so I stayed home from work the next day to put up the outside Christmas lights. I spent the morning and most of the afternoon hanging strings of marble-shaped, clear lights around the windows and borders of the house and placing nets of clear lights over the hedges. That evening, when Caleb plugged the outlet cord into the electric socket, the house and yard lit up. The Christmas season was officially underway.

We died fourteen years ago today.

Since the semester ended and she left, every minute, hour, and day has seemed longer than the one before it. Being home all day with Caleb, especially while he's in a foul mood, wasn't helping much either. It had really put a damper on my spirits, so I'd been counting down the days until Christmas. Three more days until Christmas. And four more days until this holiday season was history.

Her name was Karen Davis. Dr. Karen Davis.

I found out her name the week after the Thanksgiving luncheon. I recalled glancing at the tag on her Pathfinder the day of the luncheon, so I did a little fact finding the next week when I went back to work. I called one of my former news contacts at the Department of Motor Vehicles and had him run her tag number. That's how I found out her name. I honestly thought that I would be satisfied knowing her name, but I was wrong. Before I realized what I was doing, I was thumbing through the faculty directory. I learned a little bit more about her. She'd been a marketing professor in the School of Business and Industry for six years. She earned her Bachelor's degree, MBA, and Ph.D. from the University of Florida. But that wasn't enough, I needed more. What I really needed was to hear her voice. So I called her office. When she answered, "Hello," I apologized and said I dialed the wrong number. Hearing her voice wasn't enough either.

I'm not going to say "I told you so," but I did. Didn't I?

All I'd been able to do was think about her and wonder what she'd been doing since she'd been in Orlando visiting her parents. Every hour of the day had been filled with the same questions. Was she enjoying the holidays? Was she stressed out even though she did most of her holiday shopping before she left? Who was she spending the holidays with? Did she really care about him?

I made up my mind the day she left for Orlando. When the spring semester started in two weeks, I was going to meet and get to know Dr. Davis. I hadn't figured out how I was going to meet her, but we were going to meet.

And you wondered why Caleb had an attitude. You're either out stalking her or you're sitting here daydreaming about her. Snap out of it.

"Merry Christmas," I said and extended the gift which was wrapped in green foil and a red bow nearly as big as the box. Caleb pushed the leg rest in and rose to a sitting position.

"Thank you," he said and took the present out of my hands. "What is it?"

"Open it and see."

"I'll wait until in the morning," he said.

"No. I want you to open it now."

"Now? Tonight? Why?" Caleb asked. "We always open presents on..."

"Forget that! Just open it."

Caleb removed the bow. "You're still not getting your gift until tomorrow."

"I'm okay with that."

He undid the taped folds on one end and nudged the box from the wrapping. He hesitated before lifting the top off the box.

"A cable box?"

"It's not an ordinary cable box. We upgraded the cable channel at the School of Journalism, and we will start broadcasting some of our classes during the spring semester. This box will let you view our lectures live."

Caleb's eyes lit up. "So, I'll be in class with you...kinda?"

I nodded yes.

"Thanks." A smile, brighter than all the lights around him, illuminated his face.

"Merry Christmas, Lil' Daddy."

Lil' Daddy was a slip of the tongue. I never ever called him that. I hadn't since the accident. Caleb didn't remember our former life, so I never used the nickname Dad and Uncle Walter gave him because people said he was the spitting image of Dad. I swear it was a slip, but slip or not, Caleb heard me. He still emitted a 200-watt smile, but there was an intruding darkness dilating in his eyes.

I looked at the clock on the wall. It was seven minutes before midnight. Caleb was sitting in Dad's recliner gazing out the window. I was lying on the sofa pretending to watch *ABC's Rockin' New Year's Eve*. I tried to focus on the countdown, but I couldn't because I was possessed by an unfamiliar and worrisome feeling. Caleb was sitting in the living room with me, but I had never felt so far away from him. There was a distance between us that could not be measured in miles or breadth.

Damn. I missed it. We missed it. It's 12:02.

CHAPTER 13 ✦ CALEB

Nigel had another life, a secret life that he assumed I didn't know about.

It was past 6:30 and Nigel still hadn't made it home. I tried to reach him but couldn't. I called his office three times and his cell phone so many times that I lost count. I didn't know where Nigel could be, but when he got home, I figured he would give me some long, drawn-out story about how chaotic our day was. I wasn't wrong.

"We stopped by the library to finish the research we..." he started.

"Fuel my memory." I cut him off because I really didn't know what he was talking about. "What research?"

"Remember the article Dr. Alexander asked us to write for the department's *Outlook* magazine?"

"Not really," I responded, which was the truth because Nigel was making this lie up as he went. I didn't know why he even tried to lie because, to him, lying was like a Botox injection.

"When was this?" I asked even though I knew he was incapable of replying because his facial muscles were immobilized. "Was it before the Thanksgiving break?"

His pupils contracted. His lips stiffened. Finally, his stupefied expression earned my pity.

I pretended to recall what he was talking about. "Hold on. Wait. You mean the ethics article?"

"Yes," he uttered with slight hesitation. After he was sure that I was part of the story again, Nigel said emphatically, "The one Dr. Alexander asked us to write."

For the past couple of days, Nigel had been lying about where we've been and what we've been doing. Nigel was honest to a fault, so when he did lie, there's an earnest reason for it. At least that's what I'd made myself believe.

We always put up our Christmas tree on the first day of December. This year was different. As I sat staring at the four boxes of Christmas lights and other decoration in the living room, I debated whether or not I should put them up. The debating started around 9:00 this morning and I still didn't have an answer at 2:00 in the afternoon. Every year I went out of my way to make sure the holidays were a joyful time for Nigel. I'd seen the old photographs in the albums he kept. Christmas was once a spirited time for our family. The holiday traditions we followed were part of the memories captured in those photographs, so the holidays were a nostalgic time for Nigel.

Normally, I pulled all the lights and decorations from the closets the day after Thanksgiving, but this year I said damn it all. That's why Nigel pulled the boxes of lights and decorations out the closet before he left for work this morning. After staring at the boxes all day, I decided that I wasn't going to put up the lights and decorations. Nigel could put them up if he wanted them up.

Nigel brought a Christmas tree home when he got off work or when he finished doing whatever he'd been doing. My plan was to sit and watch him try to painstakingly recreate the Christmas tree of yesteryears, a task I can do with my eyes closed. But then

I decided to go ahead and decorate the tree. After all, I was the one who had to look at it twenty-four-seven.

We composed the final exam the way we did the midterm. But instead of discussing the wording of every question, I wrote all of the multiple-choice questions and Nigel wrote the short-answer questions and the reporter's notes for an article the students were required to write. Afterward, he looked over the questions I'd written and I did the same for him. Neither one of us had any objections. Well, at least we didn't voice them.

I called Nigel's cell phone and he didn't answer, so I left a voice message. I didn't bother to call the office since the semester was over. Although he claimed he goes to our office every day, it was obvious he was lying. An hour later, I called his cell phone again and I still didn't get an answer. So I sent him a text message: *Call me 911.* There wasn't an emergency; I wanted to see how long it would take him to call. He didn't, and he didn't drag his ass home until nearly midnight. He said the car broke down on Capital Circle. A busted radiator, he claimed.

"And we were on Capital Circle because..." I queried.

"We were on our way to the flea market." Nigel yawned. "I'm exhausted."

"We went to the flea market to look for? To buy...?"

"To just look." He squinted his eyes to feign sleepiness.

"Why?"

"No reason why," Nigel responded. "Just to have something to do."

"What time was this?"

"What time did the car break down or what time did we...?"

I cut him off. "Did the car break down?"

Nigel's calmness and bad acting faltered.

"Around four," he answered. "Give or take a half hour."

"Well, we left here at one. Where did we go?"

"We stopped by the office to check on some things." Nigel turned and looked at the clock and tried to act surprised. "Damn! I didn't know it was this late."

"I guess we got the car fixed since you drove it home."

"There's this garage not far from the flea market. One of the mechanics drove out and towed the car in. Then he patched the radiator as best as he could. Well, good enough to drive it home. They ordered a new radiator. It should be in tomorrow."

I nodded slightly.

"We'll talk in the morning." Nigel walked into his bedroom and closed the door.

Nigel didn't leave the house at all during the next few days. He sat around staring into space. I guess he forgot about the car and the new radiator that was supposedly ordered. I wasn't sure why, but something kept nagging me. Whatever Nigel did took nearly twelve hours. He'd rarely been away from home that long. Curiosity got the best of me and I decided to do a little digging. Nigel didn't like carrying a lot of cash, so the first thing I did was check Nigel's credit card purchases. We shared joint accounts so I had easy access to the information. I couldn't believe what I found out. Nigel was near Orlando the day he claimed the car broke down. He used his Visa card to purchase gas at a Turnpike travel station. Like a cockatrice, I turned and glanced at Nigel. He must have felt my virulent stare because his face hardened and his strangulating guilt nearly choked him to death. I steered clear of Nigel since then, and I didn't speak unless I was spoken to.

I knew it. I knew it. I knew it.

We needed life preservers to keep our heads above the asphyxiating waves of reticence coursing through this house. Silence swelled around us; deafening silence. We anticipated each other's every move to keep our paths from crossing. That way we didn't have to say "excuse me" or "I'm sorry" if we mistakenly bumped into each other. We used labored smiles and meager nods to say whatever needed to be said. A cursory lukewarm smile substituted for "good morning" and "good night." And a slight nod said "Thank you" or "Yes, I agree." From Nigel's constrained hush, he deduced that I was on to him. If he didn't feel guilty about what he's hiding, he would have found a way to end this strife between us.

Nigel received a letter in the mail today from a political writer for a national magazine, and he tossed the unopened envelope in the trash. Every now and then he got requests for interviews, but he still wasn't ready to talk about Barney Aman or explain why we weren't wearing Anderson Cooper's shoes.

Only God knows where Nigel had been. He rushed out of the house right before noon without saying where he was going. Actually, I didn't mind him leaving because it was the first time he'd left the house in days. Still, I was not looking forward to hearing Nigel's stitched-together fable about our day that I'd be part of to pacify him. That bothered the hell out of me. Nigel still expected me to believe him, despite the fact that he'd been lying the entire time. It's almost like he was telling me that my life outside this house was whatever he made it; that our story wasn't co-authored. However, since Nigel was out driving the Lumina, which supposedly needed a new radiator, I did have time to buy his Christmas present. I decided on a new car, a white Lexus Coupe. I was having it delivered to the house Christmas morning.

In hindsight, maybe I shouldn't have, but after I'd purchased the car for Nigel, I decided to resolve something that had been pestering me for almost two months. I tried to disregard Nigel's version of our homecoming day, but I couldn't forget the absence of the facial paralysis that signaled he was lying. He talked about navy blue, red, and white floats and bison mascots that were not in the parade I saw on television. He wasn't lying though; at least not in his mind. If he had been, I would have seen the tension on his face.

Nigel never told me, but I was aware that he had gone to college before we started at Richmond. We had a junior class schedule our first semester there. After spending twenty minutes searching several Internet databases, I found out that Nigel was a student at Howard University during our former lives and he'd pledged the Chi Alpha fraternity. Hence, it explained his knowing the Chi Alpha step dance. And Howard's mascot was the bison and its colors are navy blue, red, and white. I was relieved. For a little while, I thought my brother was losing it.

I clicked on the exit button, but the monitor flickered and jumped back to the Google search page. That's when I did what I shouldn't have. I typed in: *Richmond Times Virginia newspaper.* Forty-five seconds later, the cursor was in the archives search box of the *Richmond Times*. I counted back fourteen years; Nigel and Uncle Walter told me I was in a coma for two years and that was twelve years ago. Each keystroke felt like scaling a mountain with my fingertips…each stroke a painful step toward the peak. O - b - i - t - u - a - r - i-e-s; D - e - c - e - m - b - e - r -2-0-0-; G - r - e - e -n----. I couldn't go on. I pressed the power switch and the screen went black.

I'd never been that close to knowing what dreadful event changed our lives forever. Until now, I never wanted to know what happened to Mom and Dad. To me.

I was somebody else before that December night.

Whenever I started feeling sorry for myself, I tried to think of profound and searching words that, when strung together in the right manner, defined life's purpose. Not only my life; life in general. Sometimes, months passed without an insightful thought. And sometimes, out of nowhere, and mostly during an indifferent moment, I found reasons in the simplest of things. Seeing the color purple. The sound of music. Jazz. My brother. However, there were times when life's meaning unraveled in the sooty shadows of restless nights, when the fear of a future without me was my irascible bedfellow.

Even though I didn't feel like it, I had to write a blog. I wanted to write something about my failed search for information about that December evening nearly fourteen years ago, but I couldn't. Nigel read the blog, and I didn't want to bring up any bad memories for him. Since it was the Christmas season, I decided to write about a Christmas memory that we may have lived.

The (not so true) Way I Remember It — by Caleb Greene
Too Old For Santa?

The worst Christmas presents I ever received were the first ones I bought for myself.

I wanted to be like the other neighborhood kids my age who, because of our age, were no longer on Santa's delivery list. Even though I was twelve, I had not gone through this rite of passage and was the only person my age still waiting and wondering if Santa would bring them the perfect gift. The other kids knew what they were getting for Christmas because their parents gave them money to do their own Christmas shopping.

All my friends had been deleted from Santa's list the previous year, so I spent the entire month of December tagging along as they searched for the perfect Christmas gifts at Burdines, the Fair Store, Vera's, and Crossroads. The Calvin Klein and Cross Color jeans, the matching sweaters, and the Converse tennis shoes were all perfect fits because my friends were able to try them on before they bought them. They loved the Timex watches they got for Christmas because they'd spent several hours deciding which one they liked best. They even had the presents gift-wrapped in the paper of their choice.

I was filled with envy. Perhaps, envy is what kept me from wondering why they were at my house Christmas morning waiting for me to unwrap the Christmas gifts Santa had brought me. Or, why they kept asking if I needed help opening my gifts.

I spent an entire year anxiously waiting for the chance to do my own Christmas shopping which my mother and father opposed. However, by the time December rolled around again, I had managed to convince them I was now thirteen and too old to still be on Santa's list. They reluctantly agreed. Two and a half weeks before Christmas, a private conference was called between the three of us. During this meeting, they asked me if I was absolutely sure I wanted to be removed from Santa's list and I assured them I was. After our verbal agreement, they handed me a few crisp bills and said, "Merry Christmas."

Over the next few weeks, I wandered through nearly every store in town looking for the perfect gifts to give myself. I already knew how difficult it was shopping for someone else, but I soon learned that was a cakewalk compared to shopping for myself. For some strange reason, all the things I wanted for Christmas when my mom, dad, and Santa were doing the gift giving seemed far less appealing when I was the one handing over the cash.

I was too old for toys, but a recordable cassette player wasn't a toy, so I bought one from Wal-Mart. I purchased a pair of brown corduroy pants and a pair of jeans I wanted from Burdines. The two turtleneck shirts I bought from Crossroads matched the corduroys and jeans perfectly. And, I bought a pair of Air Nikes I'd been dying to have. After I was done with my shopping, I wrapped each one of my gifts to myself and placed them under the Christmas tree.

Bright and early Christmas morning, while my brother, Nigel, a senior in high school, was enjoying the presents Santa had brought him, I lay in bed sulking. When my mother and father asked me what was wrong, I told them I didn't know.

I guess they knew what I didn't.

The presents I bought and gave myself may have been the worst Christmas gifts I ever received, but the gold bracelet, necklace, and sweaters Santa brought me even though I was too old to be on his list turned out to be the best.

As soon as I posted the Christmas blog, the comments started. One reader asked, "Did you apologize to Santa?" Another wrote, "I became too old for Santa's list when I turned twelve. And, it was the worst Christmas I ever had." And then came the one that touched me the most. "Thanks for sharing your memories. It sounds like you had the best parents in the world," the anonymous writer wrote. I wished the memories really were mine.

On the nights leading up to Christmas Eve, we turned off the exterior and interior lights before we went to bed. On Christmas Eve, we let them burn all night. I couldn't sleep, so I stayed up with the Christmas lights, hoping to see Santa deliver Nigel's gift. His sleigh, a red and black flat-bed tow truck, stopped in front of the house at 6:30 and two of the jolly old elves' helpers backed Nigel's present into the driveway. Around 8:00, I was sitting by the window drinking a cup of hot chocolate, when Nigel walked in the living room and gestured toward the front door. He wanted to get the newspaper.

"Merry Christmas," I said and walked out of the living room.

My congenial greeting surprised him. "What did you...?" he started to ask before my courteous greeting registered. "Merry Christmas," he replied with a crooked smile.

I went in my bedroom and closed the door. I stood with my ear pressed to the door and waited to hear the front door close. When I heard the door close, I flung my bedroom door open and ran into the living room. I needed to see Nigel's reaction when he saw the white Lexus adorned with a big white bow.

His foot stopped in mid-air as he stepped down to the second step. He turned and looked for me in the window.

I pointed at the Lexus and yelled as loud as I could, "Merry Christmas!"

Nigel's feet didn't touch the ground until he was standing next to the Lexus.

"Is this really mine?"

"Yes!" I yelled. "Get in and let me see how you'll look driving it."

Nigel opened the door. The key was on the seat. He held the key up so I could see it before he sat down in the driver's seat. The Lexus fit him like a tailored glove. He loved it. But as I watched Nigel, I couldn't forget something he'd said the night before. He called me Lil' Daddy. The name Lil' Daddy felt familiar. I wasn't sure who called me Lil' Daddy, but someone did. And not any old someone. People I knew. People who knew me. They called me Lil' Daddy.

Lil' Daddy.

Lil' Daddy.

Lil' Daddy.

I was Lil' Daddy.

I started reclaiming our house the first day of the New Year. Nigel salvaged the yard. I evicted the Christmas tree this morning and Nigel dragged it outside. He said he was going to have it picked up for recycling. I packed the inside lights and decorations, then stacked the boxes in the closets. The Christmas cards from Uncle Walter and Aunt Girlie, Lillian, Professor Childers, the Hendersons, the Alexanders, and Richard Aman have been interred in the folder we kept for holiday memorabilia, and the folder was back in the file cabinet in the den. I installed the journalism department's cable box on the television. I pushed Dad's recliner back by the front window before I dusted the blades of the ceiling fan.

Lil' Daddy.

Lil' Daddy.

Lil' Daddy.

CHAPTER 14

Nigel decided that it was time they met again. Seven months ago, their paths crossed when they offered consolation to a grieving stranger. She reached out to the stranger because she felt the depth of the woman's grief. Nigel was roused to help because he knew something about the wounded woman that no one else at Barney's burial knew. Nigel guessed—because he had seen the news clipping—that the woman was Frances Pelt, and he knew Frances was mourning the loss of the man she loved and betrayed.

Their first meeting lasted a few short minutes—the time it took Nigel to convince Frances that she was not the one being buried, and for Nigel and her to walk Frances outside the gates of Springhill Cemetery.

"Thanks for helping out," Nigel said to her.

"Just doing my part," she replied. "God bless."

Those were her last words as she walked away.

There was nothing noteworthy about this first chance-upon, but afterward, Nigel couldn't stop thinking about her. During the day, he replayed his sole memory of her. Over and over, he watched her walk out of his life. And on the rare restful night, he dreamed about a life he shared with her: a life lived with two young sons in a house next to Flatley Creek. And somewhere in between, on the waning cusps of dusk and dawn, he fell in love without ever knowing her name. A little over a month ago, he saw her at a faculty luncheon. Within a week, Nigel knew her name and her office and home phone numbers. He became a patron of her favorite restaurants. He knew she worked out at Lester's Gym on Tuesdays and Thursdays. He even knew that she lived in the third house on the right on Pine Bluff Road. He was well acquainted with her from a distance, but he was ready to move in closer. Ready to touch her… feel her…and love her.

Nigel's mind was made up. They were going to meet and it wouldn't be by chance.

The sun, while bedridden with the flu, called in sick today as the dawn's chilly overcast put in overtime. It was the first day of classes and the Hill should have been teeming with students. Apparently, most chose to stay inside and forgo classes and runny noses. By mid-afternoon, twilight's early arrival triggered the outdoor lighting sensors across campus. That's when the temperature plunged.

Nigel, wearing an unbuttoned hornet-green corduroy blazer over a beige turtleneck sweater, didn't mind the gnawing cold as he walked across campus to the School of Business and Industry's parking lot west. There's a faculty parking lot outside the School of Journalism, but he parked in SBI-West to set his plan in motion. Nigel was trying to unlock his car, when he looked up and saw Karen. His Lexus was parked next to her silver Pathfinder. She pressed the unlock button on her keychain, then glanced over at Nigel and smiled. He smiled back. After trying for nearly fifteen minutes to unlock the door, Nigel conveniently remembered that all he had to do was press the unlock button on the keychain in his hand. He opened the door to get in the car, but then he stopped and looked over at Karen. She felt him staring. She put on her seatbelt, cranked the Pathfinder before turning on the heater. When she looked up, he was waving to get her attention. So, she let the window down.

"Didn't we meet at Barney Aman's...?" he asked.

"I thought you looked familiar," she answered before Nigel finished asking. "You're a reporter for the *Sentinel*, right?"

"I was."

"I saw the faculty decal on your tag. How long?"

"I started during the middle of last semester." Nigel thought he would be nervous talking to her but he wasn't. The words flowed like he had rehearsed them. "I teach Writing for Mass Communication in the School of Journalism."

"So, you're still a freshman," she said. "Welcome aboard."

"Thank you," he replied. His unfinished expression solicited, "...?"

"I'm sorry," she apologized. "I'm Karen Davis. I chair the marketing department in the School of Business and Industry."

Nigel walked over to Karen and extended his hand. "I'm Nigel Greene."

She reached out the window and shook his hand. "I really enjoyed your work for the *Sentinel*, so it's a pleasure to finally meet you."

"Meet you again," he reminded her.

Nigel studied her hand and took mental notes about its softness, how securely hers fit inside his, and how much he didn't want to release her hand. Still, the moment he sensed her hand loosening its grip on his, he let go.

She looked at her watch. "I'm running a little late, so..."

Before she could finish her statement and before he knew he was speaking, Nigel asked, "What are you doing for lunch tomorrow?"

Karen was caught off-guard. "I'm not sure." She hesitated. "Call me at my office in the morning." She put the gear in reverse. "I have a third-period class so call before ten."

"I'll do that." Nigel smiled and stepped back. "Miss Karen Davis in the School of Business, right?"

"I don't care about handles, but if you have to use one, it's Dr.

Karen Davis," she corrected him before backing out of the space.

"I'll talk to you tomorrow," Nigel shouted. He couldn't have if he wanted to, so he didn't try to harness the smile scurrying across his face as he got in his car and pulled out of the parking lot. Their second meeting had unfolded like he intended.

Karen wasn't oblivious though. She knew their second encounter wasn't purely accidental. She saw through Nigel's contrived coincidence. But there was no way she could have known that the next chapter of her life had already been written by this transparent suitor long before the spring semester began.

CHAPTER 15 ✦ NIGEL

A young lady sitting in the middle of the second row stood and announced, "I'm Toni Brown." She pulled her auburn pin braids behind her ears, then continued, "I'm from Fernandina Beach, and I'm a junior advertising major."

"Thank you, Miss Brown," I said as I walked around the lecture hall passing out the course syllabus.

The guy sitting next to Toni stood. "My name's Chris Yado. I'm a second-year pre-law major." Chris sat down and turned the Rattlers baseball cap sideways on his head.

"Thank you for removing your cap, Mr. Yado," I said. An armada of caps landed on the desktops.

The introductions continued.

This was the first session of the semester and a little over half of the seventy-six students registered for the class showed up. I figured the bad weather was to blame for the low turnout. Anyway, my assignment for the day was to have the students introduce themselves to the class, and although they didn't know it, introduce themselves to the course's co-instructor, Caleb, who was observing from his podium at home.

Caleb was where I hoped he would be—sitting in Dad's recliner, staring out the window, waiting for me. He smiled when I got out of the car, which meant he'd chilled with all the drama. Then he stood and walked toward his bedroom.

The moment Caleb heard the front door close behind me, he opened his bedroom door, darted into the living room, and cheerfully asked, "How was our day?" Before I could answer, he pounced on the recliner and said, "It feels funny asking you that when I already know how most of our day went."

"So you like the new cable system?"

"Love it, man."

"I thought you would." Caleb's eyes tracked my every movement as I put my briefcase down and sat on the sofa.

Caleb looked out the window at the Lexus. "I bet we were wildin' out on the Hill today."

"You know it." I used the remote to turn the TV to the Weather Channel. "When I went to work this morning, the campus was almost deserted. But on the way home, heads were turning."

Caleb pushed the leg rest out and reclined as we relived our day. "What did Dr. Alexander have to say?" He prepared to write himself into the rest of my day and make my day his.

Locals on the 8s was on. "We're in for a deep freeze tonight," I told Caleb.

"Whatever," he responded. "Now, what did Dr. Alexander have to say about the new ride?"

"He took a sick day, so he hasn't seen it."

Since Dr. Alexander wasn't part of our day, Caleb leaned forward in the recliner and began reflecting on our first classes of the semester.

Last week I told Caleb that the reason for my peculiar behavior during the past month or so was because I wanted to keep him from finding out about the college's new cable system before I gave him his Christmas present. I explained that I was part of the team responsible for installing the system, which meant I really was working most of the time. He bought it.

That's how our life got back to normal.

Karen and I met again today. I bumped into her in the School of Business and Industry's faculty parking lot after work. After seven months of starving for the sound of her voice, I was famished. So I devoured every word she said. She was getting ready to leave when, before I knew it, I asked her to have lunch with me tomorrow. She hesitated but she didn't say no. She told me to call her in the morning before ten. It's almost midnight, so in about twelve hours, I'd be enjoying lunch with Dr. Davis. I meant, Karen. I forgot. No handles.

I opened the curtains and blinds in my bedroom for the first time in months. I stood at the window staring at the narrow creek behind our house. Outside, the night was too dark for eyes to foresee tomorrow. The air was too cold for faith to kindle mercy. And the world was still. Nothing moved.

I was back again, standing on the banks of Flatley Creek fourteen years ago. The night was too dark to foresee tomorrow and the air was too cold for faith to kindle mercy. The world was still. Nothing moved. My feet were stuck in a fallen cloud. On one side of Flatley Creek, a trench, jagged and paneled with seared skid marks, jutted up the embankment to Stilman Road. On the side of Flatley Creek where I stood, there were two sets of footprints inscribed in the snow. The footprints started at the back door of our house and continued to the sleeted shoal of Flatley Creek. One set ended there; the set that belonged to me. The other set of footprints vanished behind the dam of shattered ice clogging the creek. An unnatural-looking pair of red water lilies illuminated the clearing in the creek. But upon closer inspection, the red lilies were the rear brake lights of a submerged car. My dad's car.

I was back in my bedroom, standing at the window, staring outside at the narrow creek behind our house. It was a little after 4 a.m. and I hadn't slept a wink. It was going to be hard to sleep, but I figured I would spend most of the night worrying about lunch with Karen instead of reliving the last minutes of my erstwhile life.

I didn't get the answer I wanted.

"I'm sorry, but I can't get away today," Karen said. "I completely forgot about a report that I have to present to the dean and steering committee this afternoon. I have to work on it as soon as I get back from class."

No was what I heard, and I didn't know how to respond because I hadn't considered the possibility that she might say no.

"Nigel? Are you still...?"

"I'm here," I promptly replied. "Sorry, I was kind of caught off guard when you said no," I explained.

"I didn't say no. I said I couldn't make it today."

She didn't say no. What she said was not today. Reassured, I suggested, "Tell you what. I don't want to keep you from your work, so I'll give you a call this time tomorrow and we'll go from there."

"That works for me," Karen answered. "Thanks for understanding."

"Thank you for keeping the lines open."

"Well, I'll talk with you tomorrow," she said and waited for me to respond. I couldn't say goodbye, so she did. Before I knew it, the phone went dead.

I rambled on about something during my third period lecture, which ended twenty minutes early. I was halfway out the door when I informed the class, "That is it for today." A few minutes later, I was placing an order at the Blue Moon coffee house near campus. At precisely 11:30, I knocked on her office door.

"She isn't here," Karen yelled from inside. "She's skinny dipping in Jamaica."

"Can you tell me how I can reach her when I get there?" I played along. "I've booked a seat on the next flight to Jamaica."

The door flung open.

"You're back?" I smiled and showed her two mocha lattes and a bag of bagels. "How about a ten-minute break?"

"Are you always this...hold on, I'm reaching for the right word."

"Call it what it is: pushy...annoying."

"All of the above and then some," she teased. "Come in." She smiled and stepped aside.

Framed family pictures were on Karen's desk and hanging on the walls. Two of the pictures were taken outside the house she'd visited in Orlando. Karen sat in the window sill and I sat in one of the three Victorian chairs in the sitting area by the window. She ate a bagel and sipped her latte as I surveyed the office and photos.

"Whose picture are you looking around for?" Karen playfully asked. "My boyfriend's?"

"I'm not looking for anything," I answered. "But since you brought him up, point him out."

"There is no boyfriend," she said. "Now, it's your turn. Are you married? I don't see a ring on your finger, but nowadays that doesn't mean a thing. And I'm being straight up when I say this. Usually, only married men are as persistent as you are. Single brothers don't waste time pursuing. If a woman isn't ready to throw herself all over him the second he smiles at her, then they brush her off like nothing and move on."

I turned and looked directly at her. "If I told you I've been waiting for this moment since the first time I saw you seven months ago, would it be okay for me to be a little bit persistent?"

From the expression on her face, she didn't know what to think of my candor. Truthfully, I was a little surprised when I heard that spring from my mouth. It came out of nowhere. But since it was out there, I asked, "Is it okay?"

"Well, if you feel like that, then go ahead and be as persistent as you want to be."

I nodded, smiling as I looked at my watch. "Nine minutes and fifty-seven seconds. Fifty-eight. Nine. Time for you to get back to work."

"I'm still eating."

"Sorry," I quipped. "Brunch is over. All I asked for was ten minutes." I started toward the door. "I'll call tomorrow morning about lunch."

"Do that."

"Count on it." I opened the door.

"Bye," she said.

I turned to Karen, who was still sitting in the window sill. "What are you doing? You have a report to finish, so get back to work. I don't want you blaming me for getting you sidetracked."

Karen stood. "I'm up."

"We'll talk tomorrow," I said and closed the door.

I called the following morning and we had lunch at Olean's, a popular cafe near campus that's famous for its Southern fried chicken and down-home cooking.

I called the next day and we spent an hour after work sitting in her office talking about Barney Aman and politics. I expected her to ask what led Barney to commit suicide but she didn't.

She called the next morning and asked what my plans were for the weekend. I told her I didn't have any. So, we went on our first unofficial date that weekend. We attended the FAMU Essential Players matinee performance of *Calming the Man*. A couple of times during the play, I glanced over at Karen and noticed her staring at me, probing for something inside me. Each time, she smiled flirtatiously and looked away.

You can't keep her a secret much longer. Caleb already suspects something after all the lies he's caught you in recently. And that lie about the report was a major blunder.

Okay! I'll tell him about Karen. He should understand.

You're right. He should. But will he?

Why wouldn't he?

Why ask a question that you already know the answer to?

Damn. This wasn't fair, I told myself.

It's not. But let's stand in Caleb's shoes for a minute, both of them. We've been standing in the right one for years. Now let's try on the other one. Is it on yet? Okay. Now, feel what he'll feel if he finds out about Karen.

He's scared.

Scared?

Terrified…

Of what?

He doesn't know what kind of life he will have if I…if I…

…if I start my new life with Karen.

What am I going to do?

Let her go.

I can't. I can't and I won't.

Then get ready. And please stop holding your mouth like that when you're lying. Believe me, it's a dead giveaway.

If nothing else, I'd always been punctual. But now, since I'd been seeing Karen, I couldn't keep track of time. This morning, I walked Karen to her office and then I had to run like a cheetah to get to my first-period class on time. I imagined the heuristic look on Caleb's face when I rushed into the lecture hall four minutes late. So far, he hadn't mentioned it, but it's on the tip of his tongue.

Karen asked me to go to a birthday dinner party for Angela Townsend, a professor in the marketing department. I was in my bedroom getting dressed when Caleb opened the door and asked, "Where are you getting ready to go?"

"To a reception for a visiting distinguished scholar."

"I don't recall you mentioning anything about a reception?" Caleb eyed me suspiciously as I looked in the mirror and straightened my shirt collar. "And I don't remember reading about this distinguished scholar. Who is he or she?"

"He's an award-winning journalist," I answered and put on my black blazer.

"Does he have a name?"

I walked past Caleb, who was standing in the doorway.

"Let me help you remember," Caleb offered as he followed me into the living room. "Is his first name John? How about Russell? Timothy?"

"Listen, Caleb..."

"No, you listen. What's up with all the lying? And I don't want to hear nothing about another project or report at work. I can't believe I fell for that bullshit the first time."

I grabbed the car keys off the table and marched toward the door. With my hand on the door, I hesitated for a moment before shouting, "I'm leaving!"

"Then leave, liar!" Caleb yelled back. "You think I give a damn?"

I turned the doorknob.

"Haul ass!" Caleb screamed. "Bye!" He stood so close behind me that I could feel the anger and hatred spewing out of him. Lava gushed from his mouth. "You're still here!"

I snatched the door open and let the world inside.

Fear chased the rage out of Caleb's eyes. He gasped. Realizing the gravity of the situation, he began to sink…to drown. His fingers clawed for the surface…for air…for me.

I walked out and slammed the door behind me. I heard Caleb fall on the floor, but I kept walking.

As I drove to Karen's house, I tried not to think about my fight with Caleb by listening to the radio and belting out songs I didn't know. She was dressed and ready to go when I arrived. Seeing her calmed my spirits. Angela and her husband, Tom, a circuit court judge, lived in Northwood Plantation. The Townsends' two-story, colonial-style log house on the shore of Lake Baldwin was a few blocks from Barney Aman's house.

I put on my best face at the dinner party, but Karen saw through it. After dinner and several rounds of evading questions from Angela, Tom, and the other twelve guests about Barney's well-publicized call to me before he killed himself, Karen asked me to walk outside with her. She reached for my hand as soon as we stepped on the deck overlooking the small lake behind the house.

"I thought you needed rescuing," she said.

"I really didn't mind."

"Of course you didn't." She moved in closer. "Thanks for coming with me."

"I'm glad you invited me," I replied. "I'm having a nice time."

"Really?"

I let go of her hand and walked to the edge of the deck. "I'm sorry." I felt the need to explain my solemn mood. "I've got a lot on my mind right now." I turned and looked at her. She was staring at the lake. "Listen, Karen."

"Sshhh." She placed a finger to my lips. "Not now. Later, when you're ready." She reached for my hand and I placed my hand in hers. "It's getting cold out here," she said and slid into my arms.

Caleb wasn't speaking to me and I didn't blame him. First, I lied to him about the report. And then, I didn't know what came over me the other night. Caleb was in bed when I came home from the dinner party, and he didn't come out of his bedroom the entire weekend...at least not while I was around. I finally saw him Monday when I pulled in the driveway after work. He was sitting by the window until he saw me. He stayed in his bedroom the rest of the night. For two weeks, I only saw him from a distance, at the window when I came home.

Caleb was sitting by the window staring outside when I pulled in the driveway and turned the car off. I didn't get out the car. I sat there and stared back at him. I wanted to see what he would do if I didn't get out. He didn't flinch; neither did I. Our standoff, which lasted twenty-six minutes, ended when I gave up. I opened the door and got out of the car. Caleb stood and walked away from the window. As I unlocked the front door, I heard Caleb's bedroom door slam shut.

I was in a terrible place and I didn't see any way out of it.

Caleb put the red envelope on the nightstand beside my bed to make sure I saw it. I ripped the envelope and the Valentine's Day card inside it into shreds, then walked in the hallway and threw the shreds at Caleb's bedroom door. "Damn you, too!" I yelled.

Karen couldn't hold it in any longer. She said she had to tell me.

"What I'm feeling or what I think I'm feeling is kind of new to me," she said. I felt her arms tighten around me as we slow danced to "Miracles," an early-eighties ballad by teen sensation Stacy Lattisaw. "I mean, I've only known you five, maybe six, weeks, and that's not long enough for me to feel like this."

"How do you feel?"

"I'd rather not say."

We were one of a handful of couples on the dance floor. Karen, a graduate of FAMU, brought me as her guest to the alumni chapter's annual Valentine's Day Ball.

"Tell me," I whispered in Karen's ear. "I want to know." I looked into her eyes and told her, "I'm listening."

"Kiss me, Nigel."

"Not until you tell me how you feel."

"Kiss me. Please."

I had a choice—continue dreaming, or live my dream. I could listen to the nervous chatter inside my head.

Don't! If you do, you'll never be able to let her go!

Or, I could pull her close and kiss her like I'd done in my restful-night dreams.

"I'm sorry," Karen apologized. "I shouldn't have put you on the spot like that." The disappointment showed in her eyes. Her grip loosened and she took a slight step away from me. "Like I said, we've only known each other a few weeks."

I missed her the moment she stepped away which was proof that I could not go back to a life without her. So I chose to live. She was spellbound by my enamored gaze as I lured her back into my arms. When our lips touched, an impassioned hunger consumed her...and me. The second chorus of Anita Ward's infectious disco hit, "Ring My Bell," had the floor gyrating when we finally realized we should be doing the Tilt, the Josie, or the Camel Walk like every-one else instead of bumpin' and grindin' like pubescent teens.

She led me up the stairs into her bedroom, then she took her time undressing me. I stood in front of her naked...harder, longer, and thicker than I had ever been. She guided my right hand toward the snap closure on the back of her strapless gown. The snap, equipped with a motion sensor, gave before I touched it. The zipper raced down her back and the gown slithered to the floor. She turned around, filled one of my hands with her warm breast. She took my other hand and piloted it inside her black lace panties. Her tongue tasted my lips before she kissed me. Her fingers tiptoed down my chest, past my navel down into my Calvins, teasingly stroking me until I throbbed. My fingers fueled a raging furnace that singed her to the core. She succumbed and fell backward on the bed. Her legs moved through the air like javelins. Her toes stabbed at the ceiling. I slid her panties up her legs and off. She wrapped her legs around my waist and steered me down on top of and in between. She invited me inside, and I fervently accepted the invitation. I felt her...all of her.

Time didn't stop. After we caught our breath and went at it again, time continued to ignore us. Even during our spontaneous romp in the shower, time pressed on, which was fine with me. I didn't want time to stop because I wanted to live every second of this dream.

CHAPTER 16 ✧ CALEB

Today was the first day of the spring semester. Nigel could come home and talk non-stop for days and never describe our classes as vividly as I saw them on TV. Now, I could be with Nigel inside SJC lecture hall, which only vaguely resembled the auditorium that I imagined. Now, I could put student faces with names when I was grading assignments and exams. I could really be there with Nigel. Be there and co-write our story. Finally, I knew what it felt like to step outside these walls…to run a marathon.

These walls, once deemed impregnable, became pervious today, and it was hard to tell where 207 Circle Drive ended and the shoreline of the world outside these walls began. It's probably my mind playing tricks on me, but I feel a nosy wind tickling my face while sand—so white and fine it resembles sugar—erect castles between my toes.

I hadn't seen Mr. and Mrs. Retired Walker since last summer, but between classes this morning, I saw Mrs. Retired Walker on the Myers Park hiking trails. I tried not to think about what seeing her without him meant. None of the hikers and joggers noticed the forlorn look on her face as they jolted by, and no one stopped to help when the excessive weight of loneliness became too heavy for her to shoulder. She completed less than a quarter of the mile-long trail before she gave up and turned around. However, she appeared content and her stride was much lighter as she followed her laden footprints back to the starting point.

Nigel was glowing when he came home, and I assumed it was due to the successful debut of the SJC cable system. He should have been excited since he was instrumental in developing it. On top of that, the broadcast allowed me to be part of our life as it was lived instead of having to be edited in later. Today was one of the happiest days of my life—of this life—and I hoped Nigel was happy for me.

Yesterday, Nigel caught me off-guard when he asked me to trim his hair. A haircut on Friday? My barbershop was open only on Sundays. It's been that way for as long as I could remember. Before I could ask why he needed a haircut on Friday, Nigel answered.

"I have to attend an important workshop on campus tomorrow, so I can't wait until Sunday."

"What kind of workshop?" I asked.

"We're meeting with a few department deans about expanding the cable system."

I figured Nigel was telling the truth because his lips didn't curdle, and he only needed two so-so breaths to serve that perfect response. Still, for future reference, I made a mental note: Weekend workshop...noted.

I began watching his every move and listening closely to every word. I even listened to his thoughts. I decided not to say anything to him. At least not yet. I kept telling myself to be patient because it would all come to light soon. Probably sooner than Nigel thought.

Nigel compiled the notes for the first week's lectures, so this week it was my turn. Today's lecture was about propaganda and mass communication. I paid close attention as Nigel presented the lesson I outlined to our first-period class. As I watched Nigel, I noticed his confident swagger as he sauntered down the aisles. During third period, I felt like I was listening to his voice and the lecture for the first time. Nigel wasn't Nigel. The guy standing in for him was engaging. Blithe. Unencumbered. He was not my brother. I was floored. Disturbed. Condemned.

I sat by the window and considered my fate.

Out there, Billy put mail in Professor Childers' mailbox, then waved as he drove past our house.

In here, fear hammered three-inch nails in the walls.

Out there, Mrs. Retired Walker began her solitary trek. Step by lethargic step, she rambled nearly two-hundred yards up the trail before she turned and headed back.

In here, I saw the rest of my life.

Nigel made it home around nine tonight. I waited in my bedroom until I heard the front door open and close, then I walked in the living room and sat in Dad's recliner. "So how was our afternoon and evening?" I asked.

Nigel set his briefcase on the floor by the sofa, then walked into the kitchen and answered, "Exhausting."

"Really?"

"We've got less than a week to finish that report about expanding the network, and..."

"Check your briefcase," I suggested.

Nigel walked in the living room and stood behind me, out of

my view, so I couldn't see what I assumed was his baffled expression. "Check my briefcase?"

I pointed at the briefcase. "Did you even open it today?"

Nigel picked up the briefcase and sat on the sofa. I watched as he fumbled with the combination lock, the apprehension evident on his face.

"Don't worry, there shouldn't be anything in there that bites," I joked.

Nigel opened the briefcase. The seventeen-page report was front and center.

"It took nearly sixty man-hours," I boasted. "Some people, like myself, take the time to do their job, while others, and I'm not calling any names, spend all their time doing whatever it is you do."

I was stunned by the look on Nigel's face as he stared at the report. It wasn't a disbelieving, or surprised, or even thankful expression. I don't know how to describe it.

I leaned forward in the recliner. "What's wrong?"

Nigel's guilt-ridden gaze answered for him. The workshops and the report were fabricated to cloak what he was really doing.

"Nigel?" I walked over to him and picked up the report. "Was all the time and effort I put into this for nothing?"

Nigel stood and slogged to his bedroom without responding. He didn't have to.

"You lied."

Nigel wasn't around even when he was here.

"What's for dinner?"

"The same thing we had yesterday. Sorry. I forgot you missed dinner yesterday, so you still wouldn't know. I suppose you could look in the refrigerator and see, but you may have forgotten where the refrigerator is."

"Caleb, I asked a simple question. Please don't make a big deal over nothing."

"Trust me. It's not a big deal. I'm saying that you're never here. Not counting the two hours you sleep and the four hours you spend plucking your eyebrows, you're here an average of three hours a day. And you spend the majority of those three hours getting dressed to leave or concocting lies about where you're going."

"I'm not here around the clock because I work."

"So do I. Wait. I forgot. You work while I sit here every day and watch you work."

"Caleb, it's been a long day, and I really don't feel like this tonight. I have apologized a thousand times for lying to you. But in case you need to hear it one more time. I'm sorry! Now let it go!"

"You ungrateful bastard! Who in the hell do you think you are? Some kind of castrated God because you get to decide my fate?"

"You really don't want to know who I am, but I'll tell you anyway. I'm a man stuck in a life that he hates! A man who detests the bullshit life he's been forced to live! That's who I am!"

"Forced? Forced?"

"Caleb, I'm sorry. I shouldn't have said..."

"Forced?"

"Caleb, please don't blow this out of proportion. You know who I am. First and foremost, I'm your brother. Your big brother. And that means..."

"Forced?"

Until today, I presumed Nigel was living a life of penance. I didn't know what happened to me and our parents, but I've always believed that Nigel was somehow responsible. That was why I never tried to talk about Mom and Dad with him. I thought he caused whatever happened, so I didn't want to bring it back up. I thought all the sacrifices Nigel made and still makes were out of obligation. That he was sharing his life with me because he destroyed mine. But Nigel said he was forced to live this life. Being forced to live a life and living a life of penance exist on opposite and parallel ends of the benevolence spectrum.

My mind had been racing and thinking inconceivable thoughts that all converged into a single assertion: If Nigel isn't living this life for atonement sakes, then he had nothing to do with the tragedy that claimed Mom and Dad. And me.

I almost died two days ago, and now I'm certain Nigel wants me out the way so he can live the rest of his life unhindered. Why else would he open the front door and let the world inside, only to stand there and watch me drown?

He said he was going to a reception for a distinguished lecturer visiting FAMU, but I knew better. I was tired of pretending to believe all the shit he had been spouting, so I told him he was lying. I didn't know whether he was pissed off over whether the truth slapped him in the face or whether the stress of trying to be here but wanting to be there had him all wired up. Whatever the reason, I'd never seen him so angry...so vindictive...so far past his end.

I'd stayed away from Nigel since he returned from wherever he went Saturday night. I heard him when he was getting dressed for work and I saw him as he backed out the driveway every morning. I saw him in the evenings when he pulled in the driveway, and I heard him stumbling around the house like he's in an unfamiliar place until way past midnight.

I'd known for years that this house was my grave. Now, I needed to know how I got here. How did I die?

This morning, Mrs. Retired Walker teetered toward the starting point of the hiking trail at Myers Park. She stood to the side and waited while others charged by. When the last procession of walkers and joggers were off and away, Mrs. Retired Walker stepped up to the starting line. She looked down the trail and smiled. She kissed her frail hands, blew the kiss into the wind, then turned and walked away, never looking back. She started down the sidewalk but stopped suddenly. She looked directly across the street at the house. She stared at the front window; at me. I could not believe it. I didn't think the Retired Walkers knew I was here watching. A smile replaced her pitiable expression as she waved. I forced a smile and waved back, realizing that I was seeing her for the last time when she turned and walked away. Before I knew it, I was unlocking the front door. I begged my hands to turn the doorknob, but my pleas went unanswered. So, I ran to the den and yanked the curtains open. Circle Drive. Towering oaks. Stately magnolias. Myers Park. People coming and going. The world was still outside my window, but she was gone from it. And that was when, for the first time that I could remember, I cried.

Yesterday forged through the barricades around 207 Circle Drive. Today, on my thirtieth birthday, I remembered being seven. I was walking from the kitchen to the living room when someone turned on a projector inside my head. I was bombarded by shards of indistinct images that knocked me off my feet. I cowered on the floor until the pictures came into focus and I realized I was recalling a real childhood memory.

I was a seven-year-old standing on a chair in our kitchen in Richmond looking inside a clear mixing bowl as electric beaters blended two sticks of butter and two cups of sugar. A box of blue birthday candles was on the table next to a box of chocolate. Mom was there. She was sifting flour in another bowl. Nigel was sitting at the table trying to make me laugh by cracking eggs into a measuring cup and pretending to eat the shells. Then Dad walked in the kitchen and kissed Mom. "I'm taking the birthday boy out back to cast a few lines," he'd said and turned his back to me. "Let's go catch your birthday dinner." I'd climbed up on his back.

I'd heard Nigel say, "Catch one for me, Lil' Daddy."

Mom had said, "I'll let you guys know when lunch is ready."

I'd waved bye to Mom and Nigel as we walked out the door and headed toward the creek behind our house.

Today, for the first time, I recalled more than a hazy face or a barely audible voice from my childhood. I remembered Mom and Dad and the sound of their voices. I remembered looking up at the cloudless sky and seeing Heaven. I remembered feeling sunlight frolic across my face. I remembered walking on grass. Joy. Life. I took out Nigel's photo albums and found three pictures of Nigel, Mom, Dad, and me on my seventh birthday. The pictures coincided with my memory. I really was seven.

Nigel stood in the hallway contemplating whether he should knock on my bedroom door. He wanted to apologize, tell me happy birthday, and give me my birthday gift. My hand was on the doorknob. I was tempted to open the door; I wanted to tell him what I remembered about my seventh birthday. Neither one of us got what we wanted tonight.

I hadn't been sick enough to need to see a doctor since we moved here, but this morning I woke up feeling something between nauseous and numb. I wondered if any doctors in Tallahassee still made house calls. The last time I actually saw a doctor was when Dr. Allen Bedford overcharged us to put me in a medically induced deep sleep and fly with me from Richmond to Tallahassee. Now that I think about it, I woke up in the same bed feeling the exact same way that morning.

A red envelope was on the table in the living room this morning. It was a Valentine's Day card from Nigel. I picked up the envelope, carried it to Nigel's bedroom, and placed it next to an unused roll of paper tape on the nightstand.

What happened?

Angela and Donald Taylor, Arnette Wilkerson, Clarence Brown, Denise Moody, Greta Lambert, Jerome Josey, and Andrea what's-her-name weren't in class this morning. Five more students were absent, but I couldn't recall their names.

Nigel's lecture was on reporting crime stories. I was watching, as usual, so as he discussed an article superimposed on a projection screen, he spoke to me with his eyes.

"After the lede, the reader knows that a masked robber walked into a convenience store with a gun and walked out handcuffed with a sore behind," Nigel explained.

His eyes told me he was sorry.

"The reader is hooked," Nigel told the class. "And now the reader has to read on."

Please forgive me, his eyes pleaded.

The students began to laugh halfway through the article.

"How stupid can you be?" Bernard Williams yelled. "Who in their right mind tries to rob a store when their mom's the clerk?"

Nigel pointed at the screen. "The article doesn't tell us if he was in his right mind, but this young man tried it."

"How come the robber's name or the name of the store doesn't appear in the article?" Mikah Cook asked.

The back door opened and Nigel looked toward the back of the lecture hall. His eyes lit up, although he restrained his smile to keep it from leaping off his face.

Another student, Ricky Jones, answered Mikah's question. "Because his parents owned the store and they asked the police to arrest him, but no charges be filed."

"Professor Greene, is that legal?" Bernard asked.

Nigel didn't respond because he had forgotten where he was.

I moved closer to the TV screen and followed Nigel's gaze.

A captivating woman, wearing a navy blue skirt and jacket, walked down to the third row from the back and sat in an aisle seat. She was too refined to be a student. She was already polished. I watched her eyes speak to Nigel. Her sunny smile kissed him.

"Can they do that, Professor Greene?" Bernard asked again.

She pointed at the screen and Nigel turned to see what she was pointing at. That's when he remembered he was in the middle of our lecture.

"Are there any questions about the article?" Nigel asked the students.

I didn't know who she was, but I'd bet anything that Nigel's new life was with her.

Nigel wasn't home, so I was alone in the dark. Every light in the house was on, but that didn't stop the darkness from creeping inside through these hollow walls and doors.

Am I more afraid of the world outside or the asphyxiating loneliness inside this house?

Nigel had never stayed out overnight, but he went out last night and didn't come home. It was almost noon and he still hadn't made it home. But, I was not going to panic or call the police because he wasn't here by choice.

There goes my life.

SPRING

CHAPTER 17 ✧

Could brothers share one life?
One world?
One love?

Spring arrived on time but, after three sprightly days on the job, Nigel decided to take advantage of some unused vacation time. Despite the guest-of-honor's absence, thousands of spectators bundled together to watch the annual Springtime Tallahassee Parade. The normally festive parade languished as local and state government officials waved gloved hands and area TV news personalities coerced smiles through shivering lips and overdressed clowns and mimes tried to mimic with frozen faces. After seeing beauty queen after beauty queen in lavish gowns and knee-length coats riding floats covered in wilted carnations and roses, Forestry Queen Jogie Brown's arrival in a confetti-colored gown with spaghetti straps was met with exuberant cheers. Young and old snatched off their jackets, gloves, hats, and tams and tossed them in the air. The gaiety spread up and down the parade's downtown route, and soon Nigel, Karen, and Caleb, who were standing on a park bench across from the courthouse, hurled their winter garb in the air.

"That felt good," Nigel said, putting his arm around Karen, pulling her closer to him.

Karen was standing between Nigel and Caleb. Most of the time,

Karen enjoyed their incessant competition for her attention, but today, she was annoyed because their antics were distracting her from the parade.

Caleb leaned over and asked Karen, "I know you've seen your share of parades, but have you ever been in one?"

"No," she answered. "But I've always wanted to. When I was a little girl, my parents took me to every parade within fifty miles of Orlando. It didn't matter what kind of parade, we were there. I always imagined that I was marching with the lead band or riding on the prettiest float."

"Well, it's time for you to march in your first parade." Caleb jumped off the bench, pulling Karen behind him, then ushered her toward the street.

Nigel lamented his decision to bring Karen into their story as he sat on the sofa watching Caleb graft himself into his morning. In Nigel and Caleb's world, a pinch of uncertainty outweighed a ton of happiness. Nigel was overjoyed at seeing Caleb so elated, so alive. But so in love? So in love with Karen? That was entirely different. For fourteen years, Nigel shared his life with Caleb, never expecting a day would come when he would have to share a woman he loved. He didn't think he would ever be in love. Still, Nigel did what he believed he had to do to stop their world from collapsing. He told Caleb about Karen. And as he sat watching Caleb, he wondered if his decision only delayed their ending.

"Where is the Marching 100?" Caleb asked as he stared at the ceiling and imagined he and Karen were watching the parade from the corner of Park Avenue and Monroe Street.

"You saw the entire parade on TV, so you know when..."

"I need you to tell me," Caleb cut him off. "So...?"

"Tallahassee Memorial's float came next," Nigel answered dryly.

"It was covered with red and white carnations. A couple of folks dressed as doctors, nurses, and healthy, happy patients rode the float."

Nigel began second-guessing his decision before the words came out his mouth. It was the day after the Valentine's Ball. Nigel spent the night at Karen's house, but he was up at sunrise and kissing her goodbye a few minutes later. He hurried home, recognizing the sobering fact that he would have to explain where he had been and what he was doing to Caleb. He drove around for hours contemplating what he would say to Caleb. It was the first time since moving to Tallahassee that he had been away from home overnight. And, although it had been weeks since Caleb even spoke to him or they were even together in the same room, Nigel was sure Caleb fretted as he sat in the black recliner by the window waiting for him. It was early afternoon when Nigel put on the right blinker, turned in the driveway, and saw Caleb sitting by the window.

Caleb spent most of the day planning and preparing for life without Nigel. He wasn't afraid. He didn't need Nigel. At least that's what he repeatedly told himself until he was convinced he really didn't. He was determined to be his own man. To stand on his own feet. To live his own life. But as soon as he saw the Lexus turn into the driveway, the thought of a life without his brother became unbearable. Debilitating. Like dying. For the second time that Caleb knew of, his tears induced a tempest and a cresting wave raced behind him as he hastened to his bedroom.

Nigel saw the dejected look on his brother's face before Caleb ran from the window. It took nearly ten minutes for Nigel to turn the key and unlock the front door and five more minutes to turn the doorknob. Anguish surged out the doorway like a tsunami and soaked him. Drowned him. Nigel panicked. He dived inside and shoved the door closed. He threw his keys and jacket on the floor as he bolted toward Caleb's bedroom.

"Caleb!" Nigel turned the doorknob, but the door was locked. "Caleb!"

Inside, Caleb sat on the floor with his back against the door. "Leave me alone," he cried.

"Open the door, Caleb."

"Get the hell out of here, Nigel. You don't have to force yourself to stay because you feel sorry for me."

"Caleb, please open the door."

"Save your pity for someone who deserves it. You didn't do this to me, so you're off the hook." Caleb's tears turned caustic. "Don't worry about me, Nigel. I'll be out of your way soon. Real soon. "

"Shut up!" Nigel kicked the door. "Shut up!" He kicked the door again and again. The lock conceded and the door slammed into Caleb, knocking him over. "Don't you ever say that again! Don't even think it!" Nigel stood in the doorway. "Listen, Caleb. I'm not here out of pity. I'm here because you're my brother." Staring into his brother's eyes, Nigel made the regrettable decision...to bring her into their life. "I'm sorry. I shouldn't have tried to keep her a secret. Her name's Karen." His confession disarmed Caleb.

"Karen?"

"Karen Davis," Nigel responded. "We met her..."

Caleb's eyes gleamed as he recalled meeting Karen at a cemetery on a rainy day last June.

Nine months later, on a frigid spring morning, Nigel tiptoed on a park bench and tried to catch a glimpse of Caleb holding Karen's hand as the two of them strutted alongside the Marching 100 in the Springtime Tallahassee Parade.

CHAPTER 18 ✧ NIGEL

I had survived, albeit barely, a constant barrage of loaded questions from Caleb since that Saturday after the Valentine's Ball.

"Yesterday, a woman walked in during the middle of our lecture," Caleb recalled the afternoon I was forced to bring her into our story. "She was wearing a blue skirt and jacket. Was that her?"

"Yes," I answered.

"I got a good look at her, and she's a Halle." A spark ignited in his eyes. "Were you with her last night?"

I nodded yes.

"So you're telling me we spent the night with her? Her?"

"Yes, but..."

"Where?"

"At her house."

Then the question that he'd asked daily for the past month arrived. "Have we...?"

"No," I snapped. "No we haven't! And I don't care if you don't believe me."

"Why wouldn't I?" Caleb asked with a wry grin.

I saw a light—a fiery beacon of possibilities—in Karen's eyes, and I was gluttonously drawn to it.

"Good love," Karen replied as we recovered from an impromptu late afternoon tryst in her bedroom. "I wanted to know what good love felt like."

"What do you mean, good love?"

"When we met, I already knew you were a man with high morals. Remember, you quit your job to preserve another person's dignity. You're caring and you live by principles, which means you would love a woman like she should be loved." Karen gently pressed her body against mine. "There's still a lot that I don't know about you. But I know that your feelings are sincere. And your love is good."

"Is that the only reason you...?"

I think she sensed my quandary.

Karen leaned over and propped up on my chest. "Don't get the big head, but you're kinda cute, too."

"Cute?"

She whispered in my ear, "Cute in a stallion, you know, stud kind of way." Her tongue glided across my earlobe and then down my neck. "And you taste good. Really, really good."

"Don't," I begged. "Ooohh. Don't do that. I have to go. I can't. Damn. It's getting late."

"It's only 7:30."

"I know, but..."

"Don't," she stopped me. "You don't have to." She rolled over to her side of the bed.

"I'll call you tomorrow," I said.

She acknowledged with an insipid smile.

I sat up on the edge of the bed. I was about to stand, when suddenly, I found the courage to ask Karen another long-simmering question. "How come you never ask about my life away from work and here?"

Karen didn't respond, so I turned around and looked at her. She sat up, gazed into my eyes, and said, "I know you're living two lives, and I know that your other life has nothing to do with loving another woman."

"How did you...?"

"By looking at you," she answered. "I saw it the day after we met. Remember? You stopped by my office with brunch."

I was finally ready to let her know me. Know my life. "Well, aren't you a little curious...?"

"I'm extremely curious. I'm talking dying-to-know curious."

"Then why do you always stop me whenever I try to talk about my personal life?"

"Honestly?"

"Please."

"Because I love you, Nigel."

I'm alive. I'm alive.

"I see you," she revealed, "and I feel the sadness you live with. You do your best to conceal it, but it's so ingrained in you that you can't. I see it. I feel it. And sometimes it scares me."

"Scares you?" I asked. "Why?"

"Because I don't know how to help you," Karen answered. "But don't worry. It scares me, but not enough to make me stop loving you. Like I said..." She wrapped her arms around me. "Your love is good."

I'm going to live forever.

I was so blissfully inebriated that Karen had to help me put on my clothes. When she finished dressing me, she kissed me good-bye, then sent me home to my other life.

She loves me. She loves me. She loves me. She loves me. She loves me. She loves me. She loves me. She loves me.

I was a chassis—a man with no heart, no spirit, nothing inside—when I was not with her. But I couldn't be with her too much; the more time I spent with Karen, the more Caleb expected to participate in and hear about our relationship. Lately, when we discussed our day, he fast forwarded through the majority of it. He was only interested in hearing about the time I spent with Karen. Usually, I told him as much as I could without divulging anything about our intimate moments. As I recapped my day, Caleb joined Karen and me for lunch, dinner, movies, walks across campus, and even a few content-edited quiet moments. After he was done making my day his, he always asked in an obviously suspicious tone if we had sex with Karen. My answer was always no. I couldn't and I wouldn't ever tell him that Karen and I make love two, maybe three times a week. I refused to share that part of her.

I missed my secret life with Karen—when I didn't have to concede part of her to my brother, Caleb. Now, the only time I was alone with her was when we're having sex.

I admired Dr. Alexander. He had been happily married for nearly twenty years, and he wore this beatitude of marriage, family, and achievement like a royal crest. Even still, his matinee-idol looks and jovial demeanor caused women to be irresistibly drawn to him. Always amiable, he dismissed their flirting in a manner so inconspicuous that most strutted away with a renewed faith in men, kittenish smiles, and attentive nipples.

Yesterday, while we were having lunch at a sandwich shop near campus, I asked him about his secret. "Why are women so attracted to you?"

"I didn't know they were," he replied with a grin.

"Sure you didn't."

"Well, if that's true…and I stress the word, *if*…then I think it's because they sense I'm unavailable. And people, men and women, have a tendency to covet things that are out of reach."

That's when I told him about Karen. He wasn't surprised though. He said he noticed something was different about me right after the semester began, and it took him a few days to deduce what it was. I walked lighter.

This morning, after I finished giving mid-term exams, Dr. Alexander stopped by my office and invited Karen and me on a crabbing trip. "Gloria and I are going crabbing Saturday morning," he said. "And, if we catch anything, we're having a backyard crab boil that afternoon."

"I've never been crabbing, but it sounds like fun," I told him. "I'll talk to Karen and let you know tomorrow."

"Good." Dr. Alexander started toward the door, but stopped and turned around. "I haven't met Karen, but I can look at you and tell she's good for you." He opened the door. "My advice to you is, let yourself be happy. Happiness isn't a bad thing."

I immediately took his advice. "What time are we leaving Saturday?"

"Six thirty." Dr. Alexander smiled affably. "Good man." Then he closed the door behind him.

Caleb wasn't at the front window when I pulled in the driveway and parked beside the Lumina. I knocked on the front door and yelled, "I'm coming in." I opened the door wide enough to squeeze inside and slammed it closed. I set my briefcase on the sofa and called Caleb. He yelled for me to come to his bedroom. I knocked before opening the door. Caleb was hanging a framed picture of Karen on the wall. He said he printed the photo off the School of

Business and Industry's web site. He stepped back and inspected his work, then he asked me what I thought about the picture. "It's her," I answered and walked out the room.

Caleb was in love with Karen. I couldn't blame him though. What man wouldn't love her? However, that didn't mean I was okay with him being in love with a woman he'd never met. I couldn't tell him how I really felt because he'd swear he saw jealousy rearing its vile head.

Karen, wearing nothing but a lavender blouse, was sitting on the desk when I opened the door and stepped in my office. I reached for the light switch.

"Don't," she purred. "Close the door and lock it." She uncrossed her legs. "Now, come here."

"What's going on?" I asked as I walked over to the desk. She used my tie to tow me into position between her legs. She kissed me. "Karen...?"

"You said you couldn't wait," she answered. "Neither can I." Karen unbuckled my belt, then she unbuttoned my pants and shirt. I stood there like a mannequin. "What's wrong?" she asked. "I've seen you naked before." She stuck her hand inside my boxer briefs and began stroking me. "Damn! A girl can get hooked on all this."

"Are you forgetting where we are?"

"In your office," she replied and unsnapped the lone button on her blouse. I was fascinated with her breasts, and my hands were cupped around them before I knew it. She wrapped her arms around my neck and her legs around my waist. Then she lay back on the desk, taking me down with her.

I wasn't sure which one of us knocked the phone and answering machine off the desk, but I was stupefied when a recorded message began playing. "Nigel," the caller said, "it's Karen. Thanks for the flowers. How did you know tulips were my favorite? They're beautiful. And so you know, I feel like skipping class too, Mr. Greene. Call me."

What flowers? I didn't send any flowers.

"How did you know?" she asked and motioned for me to roll over on my back. I did. She climbed across me, straddled me, then eased her way down.

That's when it hit me. *"Caleb!"*

Her sudden pause was nearly undetectable, but my out-of-nowhere stammer almost ended the moment for me.

Karen recognized my blunder and quickly went about rekindling the passion. "Don't stop," she begged. "Please don't stop!"

I put my hands around her waist and ravished her body. "Who do you belong to?" I asked.

"You! I belong to you," she feverishly declared. "I'm yours Nigel! Yours!"

"All mine?"

"Ooohh yes!" she erupted. "All yours!"

"You're home early," Caleb said as he emerged from his bedroom.

I dropped my briefcase on the floor. "Caleb, you shouldn't have done that." Caleb's eyes widened. I looked right at him, and without flinching, I let him know, "She's my girlfriend. Not yours."

"The card was signed, Mr. Greene, so she thinks you sent the flowers."

"That's beside the point." I needed to calm down so I sat on the sofa. Caleb walked over to the recliner and sat. "You shouldn't be feeling like that about her," I explained.

"Why?" Caleb leaned back and pushed the leg rest out. "I already know why, but I'm asking you. I want to hear you say it." Caleb's lips drew tight as his fingers tapped a jagged melody on the arm rest. "Why shouldn't I feel like this about her?"

I considered what I wanted to tell him and what I was going to tell him. I wanted to say, *she's mine. She doesn't even know you exist. So leave us alone.* What I ended up saying was, "Forget it. I want to know what was written on the card."

Caleb relished the moment. He thought he knew why I was so angry.

"Beautiful. I can't wait until tonight," Caleb gladly revealed. "I need you right now. Let's skip class. Mr. Greene."

"That's it?"

"That's it," he answered. "Short and simple gets them every time." Caleb's eyes gloated. "So did you?"

"No!"

"Hey, I'm simply asking."

Caleb didn't believe me, so I pressed on. "How did you know tulips were her favorite flower?"

"Angela Townsend told me."

"How do you know Angela?"

"I don't. I looked in the faculty directory and called two of Karen's female colleagues in the marketing department. I said I was you and that I wanted to surprise her by sending a bouquet of her favorite flower. The other lady didn't know, but Angela told me, well me as you, that Karen really likes tulips."

I was angry. Insecure. And, I wasn't ashamed to say that I was jealous. I had a right to be. I may have reaped the benefits, but it was Caleb's words that turned her into Mt. St. Helen. He filled her with a heated passion I'd never felt in her. She was ready to erupt. Caleb knew what he had done and sat there smiling victoriously like he had sex with her. I had to get up and go to my room before I put my foot in his behind, so I muzzled my thoughts, stood, then headed for my bedroom.

"Dinner will be ready in about twenty minutes!" Caleb yelled.

I slammed my bedroom door so hard that a picture fell off the hallway wall. I heard the frame hit the floor and the glass shatter. A minute later, I heard footsteps in the hallway and the marring sound of glass being swept across the hardwood floor.

"If Mom was here," Caleb said loud enough for me to hear, "you'd have a raggedy ass for slamming that door like that."

"Mom?" I was floored. Caleb said something about Mom. Fourteen years and he'd never said anything about her. And then, in that instant, he said, "Mom?"

I willed myself to open the door.

The cracked frame holding the picture of Mom at her surprise birthday party was on the floor. I was in a daze as I stood in the doorway watching Caleb sweep the broken glass onto a dustpan.

"Nigel, do you remember when we helped Mom bake my birthday cake?" Caleb asked, walking into the kitchen. He emptied the dustpan in the garbage before returning to the hallway. "Dad took me fishing out back while you finished helping Mom." Caleb's expression was illegible. His smile, cloaked. His eyes, hollow, barren. "I can still see Mom lighting the seven blue candles on my chocolate cake. Do you remember, Nigel?"

Remember? I couldn't remember. Not while the calamitous hush of utter disbelief rang in my ears. I was straddling time. Standing in three places at once: a hallway inside 207 Circle Drive; the shoal of Flatley Creek on a December night fourteen years ago; and in the kitchen of our childhood home watching our mother put seven blue candles on a chocolate birthday cake. In each place and time, I was shackled by fear as I watched our lives change forever…again.

"Hey, Uncle Walter." The last time I called Uncle Water was Christmas Day, but I woke up this morning needing to hear his voice. "It's me. Nigel."

"I know who it is. I'm not so old and senile that I've forgotten my nephew's voice. Believe it or not though, I was telling Girlie right before you called that I was going to call you and Caleb this afternoon. You've been on my mind quite a bit here lately. So, tell me what's going on. Is Caleb all right?"

"Caleb's okay. I called to hear your voice."

"How much time you got?"

"All day," I responded.

"Then kick back," Uncle Walter said. "We've got some catching up to do."

I lived with Uncle Walter and Aunt Girlie during the two years Caleb was in a coma because Uncle Walter was vehemently against me living alone in my parents' house. His stance didn't change when Caleb was released from the hospital, but he agreed to support our decision on a trial basis. The day before Caleb came from the hospital—the day before we moved in—I locked and sealed the back door. During the two and a half years we lived there, I never unlocked the back door or set foot in the back yard or anywhere near Flatley Creek's hollowed bank.

I knew memories were going to kill me one day. When people ask what dreadful accident or illness took me out, I pray Caleb doesn't tell them I was slain by the memory of seven blue candles on a chocolate birthday cake.

CHAPTER 19 ✦ CALEB

"Barney died," Nigel told Barney Aman's dejected lover, Frances Pelt, whose feet had taken root in the desiccated dirt around Barney's grave.

"Not you," I finished Nigel's assertion, then reached for her hand. Nigel gripped Frances' other hand, and we lifted her out of the makeshift crypt inside Barney's.

Then suddenly, and I mean out of nowhere, this heavenly vision appeared and covered Frances, Nigel, and me with her umbrella. "Thanks," Nigel and I turned to her and said. Her subdued smile snagged our hearts and hypnotized us as we led Frances past the curious stares and the muffled whispers, through the wrought iron gates of Springhill Cemetery, to the Bonneville that would transport her back to a life created by retaliation and governed by remorse.

Nigel and I thanked her again and she replied, "Just doing my part." That was all she said before vanishing like she appeared.

I know it sounds bizarre—meeting the woman of our dreams while exhuming Frances from Barney's grave—but that's exactly how it happened.

Seven months came and went before we saw the Good Samaritan again. Then one afternoon last month, we happened to bump into her on campus in the faculty parking lot. If memory serves me right, it was the first day of the spring semester.

I drank a cup of black coffee and read the newspaper between classes. As usual, I started with the obits. I never knew Mrs. Retired Walker's real name, so with my fingers crossed, I scrutinized the obituary of every woman in her sixties or seventies to see if something written about the deceased women would catch my attention: *A resident of the Myers Park community; Preceded by her husband, who passed a year ago; She was an avid walker.* There were no flags today, which left me relieved and convinced that Mrs. Retired Walker merely grew tired of living alone, sold her house, and moved back to her childhood home in Bountiful.

Public affairs reporting was the topic of today's lecture. I sat through first period, so I'd heard the lecture. I sat through third period too because I was hoping Karen would stop by like she did last week. While I sat there waiting for her, I wrote this week's blog. And since I couldn't think of anything but Karen, I wrote about her.

The Way It Is – by Caleb Greene
Falling In Love
If you're reading this, you've probably already noticed that the name of this week's blog has changed. "The (not so true) Way I Remember It" is now "The Way It Is." But, don't worry. It's only a temporary change. Why? Well, it's because this week's blog isn't about a memory I wish I had lived. Instead, it's about the memories I hope to make now that I'm falling in love.

That's right. I'm falling in love. And, believe it or not, this feeling is new to me. It's my first time falling in love. At least, it's the first time that I can remember. I'm guessing that because I'm a fairly good-looking

*guy (if I must say so myself), I'm cool, and I've got plenty of swagger,
that somewhere back in my forgotten past, I had my share of admirers.
So maybe I fell in love with the prettiest girl at my high school or maybe
she was the girl next door. I don't remember. And since I don't remember,
I feel like I'm falling in love for the first time.*

*Her name is Karen and it was love at first sight. I knew I loved her
the moment I laid eyes on her because I saw my life change before my eyes.*

*Until I met Karen, I had given up on ever finding love. Actually, I can't
say I had given up, because I'd never thought about being in love. I
didn't think there was a place for love in my life. Thankfully, I met her.*

Karen! Karen! Karen!

*I'm gushing, aren't I? I can't help it. Like I said, these feelings are all
new to me.*

*When I'm with her, I never want to leave her side. When I'm not
with her, I can't stop thinking about her. So, one way or the other, she's
always with me.*

*I know that it's love because the very thought of her can turn a bad day
into an unforgettably brilliant day. She has that kind of an effect on me.*

*We have such a great time whenever we're together. We were at the
Springtime Tallahassee Parade and she told me she had always dreamed of
marching in a parade. I responded by telling her that we were at a parade,
so all we had to do was march. The next thing I knew, we were marching
alongside the bands and floats in the parade.*

*There is one problem though. I'm acting like a sixteen-year-old falling
in love for the first time, and I know that it's driving my brother Nigel
crazy. He hasn't said anything, but he keeps looking at me like he wants
to say, "You're embarrassing me. Now, grow up." And, maybe I am. But
you can't blame me. I've never been in love.*

I'm falling and I don't want to get up.

Enough said.

I couldn't wait to read the comments about this week's blog. The comment I wanted to hear most was the one that wasn't coming: the one from Nigel. He'd commented a few times in the past, so I figured Nigel would read the blog, but I was also sure that he wouldn't say a thing to me about it.

Nigel really liked Karen. That's why he started to see me as competition.

Karen didn't show up during third period, which meant I wasted an hour sitting here listening to Nigel's rambling.

Nigel and I were both thirty-four in the waist, so his pants fit me fine. The problem was the length. The cuffs were an inch above my ankles. Same went for his shirt and jacket. I tried on the charcoal Armani suit he wore to the Valentine's Ball Friday night—the night he spent with Karen. I could still smell her perfume and feel her touching us. The thought of being that close to her aroused emotions that I'd never felt. An intense awakening undressed me in the living room and sent me sprinting to the shower. I was so hard it hurt. I wrapped my hand around my throbbing penis and I tried to make love to her. Damn. Damn! Damn! I couldn't do it. I couldn't. Not then. I had to wait.

Was I still a virgin? Maybe I had sex before this life. Did I? I wish I could remember.

I still couldn't believe Nigel went shopping at Governor's Square Mall. I was sitting by the window when he pulled in the driveway this afternoon. The back seat and the trunk were packed to capacity. It took him three trips to bring all the bags inside. Then he separated them into two mounds on the living room floor. Thirteen bags in his pile and eleven bags in mine.

"What's the occasion?" I asked.

"Spring," he answered. "I hope you like what I picked out."

I opened a bag from Dillard's. "Three Nautica shirts and two pair of shorts. How much did you spend?"

"Not that much?"

I closed the bag and opened a bag from the Gap. I saw the receipt first. "One-hundred, sixteen dollars! How much is not that much?"

"All together, a grand and a half."

"Are you crazy?"

"Yes," he proudly declared. "Crazy in love."

I didn't want to say it and I tried hard not to, but my spiteful side won out. "Me too," I proclaimed.

Nigel would never say it, and he assumed I didn't know it, but he hated having to share Karen with me.

Karen was a godsend. She gave us a real life. We became more than onlookers. More than walking, breathing, animated specters. We were really alive. I loved our new life, and I would have done anything to keep from going back to our old life.

Nigel, Karen, and I ate dinner at Karen's house Wednesday night. We had planned to go out, but then Karen decided she would cook dinner and we could hang out around the house. Karen cooked the best lasagna I've ever tasted. She said she found the recipe handwritten on the inside back cover of a copy of *The Godfather* that she bought at a yard sale. Anyway, we were discussing how much Tallahassee had grown over the past few years, when she commented on all the changes Orlando, her hometown, was under-going when she was home in December. She asked if we had ever been to Orlando and I immediately turned and looked at Nigel. We both answered no. I was telling the truth, and Nigel's incul-pable expression nearly had me convinced he was telling the truth even though I knew better. I scribbled a mental note.

Nigel was in the Orlando area in December.

Every morning I woke up with a massive hard-on pitching my blanket like a teepee. I was getting desperate now, and I didn't know how much longer I could fight this feeling. It took all of me to deny myself this morning, like yesterday and the day before that. The reason I couldn't seem to think of anything but making love to Karen was that Nigel kept that part of her from me. He kept saying he hadn't made love to her, and I kept pretending to be-lieve him.

"Hello. You've reached the office of Karen Davis," the voice recording announced. "I'm away from my desk, so please leave me a message."

Karen was in class. I called to hear her sultry voice on the an-swering machine.

Dr. Alexander asked us to call him Hubert.

"We're wading in the gulf, tying string to raw chicken wings, and you're calling me Dr. Alexander. Off campus, I'm Hubert. Besides, I don't hear you calling Karen, Dr. Davis."

"That's because she told me that she doesn't care for handles," Nigel explained.

"Don't argue with him," Gloria butted in. "This is the first time I've heard my husband tell someone not to address him as Dr. Alexander. This is a breakthrough."

It was Saturday morning and we made our way through Hickory Mound, near the mouth of the Econfina River in Taylor County. We parked and set up in a clearing near a large drainage pipe. We began by tying chicken wings to six strings and tying the other end of the strings to wooden stakes that we mounted in the ground. Karen and Gloria tossed the chicken bait in the water and tended to the strings, while we walked along the edge of the tea-colored water trying to scoop crabs from the shallows with our nets. Nigel and I acted like two clowns the first time Karen yelled she had a crab on one of her strings. We nearly broke our necks racing over to her. And in our haste, we scared the hell out of everything in the water. It was two hours before we spotted another crab. After Nigel netted that one, it turned into a free-for-all. By noon, our cooler was full.

Around that time, the lunch bell rang and swarms of sand gnats, mosquitoes, and yellow flies smacked their lips and said grace. We packed in a hurry and headed back to Tallahassee. Hubert dropped us off on campus where Karen's Pathfinder was parked, and we followed him to his house. There, we spent the afternoon listening to old school music, drinking Heinekens and Crown Royal, and pigging out on garlic crabs, potatoes, corn on the cob, and smoked sausage. I ate and drank until I was miserable. Around seven, when the mosquitoes crashed the cookout, we said bye to the Alexanders and thanked them for the good time. We drove to Karen's house where we parked the Lexus that morning, kissed Karen good night, then checked back into 207 Circle Drive. It turned out to be a Saturday well spent.

I couldn't keep my eyes off Karen today. When she looked at me, it felt like she was looking inside me. And the smile on her face said she liked what she saw. Yes, she's my brother's girlfriend, but I couldn't turn this feeling off. I wanted to put my arms around her and hold her next to me. I wanted to kiss her. Make love to her. Be hers.

I asked Nigel why Karen never called him here at home. He said she called him on his cell phone whenever she wanted to talk. I asked him if she knew the number here. He said he didn't know. I asked him had he given her the number here. He said no. I asked why. He said because she never asked for it.

The tulips did the trick.

Nigel came home early from work today. He was obviously ruffled. His face was flushed. His hair was hand-brushed into place. His heart was defiled and filled with a jealous rage. He was blunt, leaving no room for discussion. He told me to stay away from Karen and to stay out of his love life.

"Listen, Caleb, I'm only going to say this one time. I want you to stay away from Karen and I want you to stay out of my love life. Do you hear me?"

"What brought this on?" I asked and waited for him to tell me what happened when Karen received the tulips, but he didn't say anything about taking a midday recess to quench the fires I ignited in her. He didn't have to. I already knew.

"Don't worry about what brought it on," Nigel responded. "Just stay away from us. I won't tell you again."

I'd never been the type you could bully, so I stood and looked directly at Nigel. "Are you asking me or telling me?"

"Telling you," he replied.

"And if for some reason I didn't quite hear you or I don't give a damn, what's up?"

I thought Nigel would back down, but he didn't.

"Try me and see," he answered.

I wasn't ready to back down either, so I walked up to Nigel and stared him in the eyes. "Would you call this trying you?"

"Yeah, I'd call it that," he said.

"So?" I solicited.

Nigel shoved me in the chest, and I stumbled backwards and fell back on the sofa. I jumped up and was about to kick Nigel's ass, when I saw the welcoming look on Nigel's face. There was a long-time-coming smile on his face that signaled he was ready to release the years of pinned up anger and frustration on me.

Nigel urged me on. "Come on. What's the hold-up? Bring it."

I quickly rethought my plan. Nigel and I had never fought, but in my mind, I always figured I could beat him if we did. But, the way he was looking, I wasn't sure. And, I wasn't ready to take any chances. So I turned and walked over the recliner by the window.

"I didn't think you were up to the task." Nigel turned and walked to his bedroom. He slammed the door shut.

I went to bed around nine o'clock, hours earlier than I usually turned in. I thought I was ready, but my nerves got the best of me. I didn't trip out though. After all, it was going to be my first time, and I didn't want to rush things.

It was a little after midnight, and I was standing in our office when the door opened and she walked in. Except for a tulip she used to caress her breasts, we were both naked. She handed me the tulip, then she turned around, placed her hands on the desk, and beckoned for me. I walked up behind her and waited for her to invite me in. Her smile told me to let myself in, and I replied, "Gladly."

I was sure Nigel and Karen's first time didn't happen here, but I was certain they made love here today. My first time, or at least the first time I remembered, was everything I imagined it would be. We made love. Tender. Passionate. Reckless love.

During our second round, I sat in my desk chair and she sat in my lap, facing me. Our lips and body fused in ways I never thought possible.

Our third go at it was on top of the desk around 4 a.m.

At 5:30, we fell asleep in each other's arms.

Forty minutes later, my alarm clock rang and I awoke to a brand-new world.

I'd never wanted to live and walk outside these walls as much as I did today. But as I sat here elated, I felt a tinge of envy toward Nigel because he was able to touch, feel, and know her. Touching, feeling, and knowing her made their love real.

I spent spring break watching nervously as Caleb rediscovered our former life. Karen asked me to spend the break with her down in Orlando, but I passed. I couldn't be away from home for an entire week. Especially not now…he was close.

As much as I hated to admit it, I'd been out of whack since Caleb sent Karen the tulips and since I read his blog about falling in love with her. I couldn't believe that I let jealousy make me want to fight him. Since that day, two incendiary questions held my future hostage. If Karen met and got to know Caleb, would she be more attracted to him? I hated myself for being so insecure about love and women. I'm thirty-five, not sixteen. I should know what I was capable of by now. Which brought up the second question: shouldn't I know what I was capable of?

I read somewhere that dreams were a reflection of our subconscious thoughts, and I hoped that wasn't true. I read Caleb's blog about falling in love with Karen while I was at work the other day, and that night I had a dream that Caleb and I really did get into it about Karen. He didn't back down in the dream like he did in real life.

In the dream, like in real life, I was sitting at my desk reading Caleb's blog. I wasn't surprised that he had fallen in love with Karen. After all, we shared my entire life. Why wouldn't he want to share my love for her? I asked myself that question in real life and in the dream. In the dream, as in real life, the possible answers had me boiling over inside. It pissed me off that I had to share her with Caleb, and I let myself feel it. By the time I finished reading the blog I picked up my briefcase and marching out of the office. I was ready to tell Caleb how I really felt about him falling in love with my woman.

I was sitting in our driveway before I realized I had made it home. In the dream, Caleb must have been telepathic, because he stood in the window waiting for me with a smirk on his face. In real life, he was standing in the window when I got home, but I don't think he had the smirk on his face or at least I didn't see it. That's why I didn't walk in the house ready to kick off in his ass like I was in the dream. Caleb had the smirk on his face in the dream knowing I was going to read the blog, and he guessed how pissed off I would be, especially after he sent her the tulips. He didn't care though. He was as ready to fight over her as I was.

I hurried out the car and slammed the door closed. Then, without looking up at the window where Caleb was still standing, I walked around the car and toward the front door. Usually, I took my time about unlocking the front door and going inside to make sure Caleb had time to go to his bedroom before I opened the door. In the dream, I didn't waste any time. I had the key out when I stepped up to the door. I inserted the key, turned it, and pushed the door open.

Caleb wasn't in the living room.

I stood in the doorway with the door opened and let my anger build. My anger had subsided slightly during the drive from campus to home, but I think seeing the smirk on Caleb's face re-ignited it. I took my time about closing the front door, but as soon as it was closed, I turned and announced, "The door's locked!"

Caleb wasted no time opening his bedroom door and stepping into the hallway. "Yeah, it is. And…?" he asked in a sardonic tone.

"And it's whatever you got on your mind, little brother," I replied and dropped the briefcase on the floor.

Caleb took deliberate steps as he marched up the hallway toward the living room. "Seems like you're the one with something on your mind," he said.

"Yeah, I have something on my mind," I responded as I walked toward him.

"Then get it off." Caleb stepped right up to me.

I didn't back down. "I should get it off, shouldn't I?" I didn't blink as I stared back into his eyes.

Caleb didn't back down either. "I would if I were you."

"I read your blog," I told him.

"And?" he asked.

"And she's mine."

"Says who?"

"I said she's mine. Now, get rid of the blog."

"Make me."

I swear I didn't know I was going to swing, but my fist slammed into Caleb's jaw before I realized it. Caleb staggered backward and fell on the sofa. As I stood staring in disbelief, Caleb jumped up from the sofa and charged into me, knocking me backward on the floor. The fall knocked the breath out of me, and I landed on my back with him straddling my chest. I tasted the blood gushing from my lips after he jabbed me twice. Finally, I managed to gather my senses. I grabbed my briefcase, which was on the floor beside me.

"I've been waiting to do this for ten years," Caleb said, then grabbed my collar. He was about to hit me again when the brief-case careened into his head. He fell on the floor beside me, and I hurried to my feet.

"Get up!" I yelled. "Get up!"

Caleb scrambled to his feet, and as soon as he stood, I tackled him. We landed on the sofa and the sofa flipped over on top of us.

That's when I woke up with my fists balled up so tight that my fingernails were cutting into my palms. It took more than just a few minutes for me to calm down. I read somewhere that dreams are a reflection of our subconscious thoughts, so I decided not to allow myself to dream anymore that night by taping my eyelids open.

"Ouch!"
That's what I got for running out of paper tape.

Karen was in the faculty parking lot waiting for me when I arrived on campus this morning. She walked up to the car as I got out and jokingly asked, "Who arched your eyebrows?"

I closed the door and pressed the lock button on my keychain.

"I'm sorry. I shouldn't have said that," Karen apologized, then reached for my hand.

I pretended not to see her extended hand. "I have a meeting with Hubert, so I don't have time to walk you to your office."

She continued holding out her hand. "Nigel, is something wrong?"

"No. I have this meeting and..."

"Don't let me keep you," she cut in.

I stepped past her outstretched hand and began my trek to the School of Journalism. I hated lying to Karen, but I'd rather lie and avoid her than let her see me like this. Jealousy was making me crazy. I know Caleb hadn't really had sex with Karen, but I'd bet my life that in his mind, he'd been with her every day since he wooed her with the tulips.

Between first and third period, I walked over to the campus parking office and changed my decal back to the School of Journalism's faculty parking lot. When I returned to my office, I listened to three messages from Karen. Two were left on my cell phone's voice mail. The other was on the office phone's answering machine. The messages were all the same. "Call me when you get a chance." I deleted the messages and turned off my cell phone.

Karen wasn't waiting for me in the parking lot this afternoon. Her Pathfinder was still parked next to my car, but she was nowhere in sight. I was slightly relieved. As I drove out the parking lot, I glanced in my rearview mirror and saw her. She was standing in the shadow of a maintenance building waiting for me to leave.

I had to choose. So I chose the life I couldn't live without and cremated the life that made me want to live.

Withdrawal cravings wouldn't let me sleep. I needed to hear her voice, see and feel her. Make things right again. I conned my fingers into dialing her number on my cell phone, but no matter how much I enticed them with the promise of touching her, I couldn't persuade them to press the send button.

During an interview a few years ago, a local author of self-help books told me that it takes approximately twenty-one days to break a habit. So, in twenty-one days, I would have forgotten her. I looked at the clock; it was 4:30. I reminded myself that I could write day one off if I could make it through the first night.

It finally dawned on me why I fell in love with Karen the moment I saw her at Barney's burial. Her quintessence gleamed like a celestial flare. She was beautiful. Kind. Alive. And she was complete. There was no longing in her heart, because she owned all of her tomorrows. She was alive. And I saw what my world could be like with her in it.

I was content with our life until the possibility of another life dangled in front of me.

Day five and counting.

I expected her to call, or show up at my office, or pull in the driveway and knock on my front door. I expected her to do something. Anything. But she didn't. It's the eighth day and I hadn't seen or heard from her. It's like she said, "to hell with Nigel." Talk about adding to my insecurity.

Caleb wasn't interested in my day anymore. Most of the time, he's waiting for me to get home so he could quiz me about one of his newfound memories. Today, he questioned me about the weekend when the entire family helped me move into the freshman dorm, Rawlings Hall, at Howard University. It wouldn't be long before he remembered how we died on the shoal of Flatley Creek three years later.

I kept hearing Barney ask me, "Have you ever really loved someone?" Now, I could answer him truthfully. Yes. Yes. Yes. Yes.

I didn't want to be the man who sullied Karen's heart, but I had to find a way to stop loving her. I'd convinced myself that I'd done the right thing by protecting my brother and saving our world.

Day thirteen didn't count; I backslid. I had not driven the Lumina in four months, but I decided to take it for a spin after dinner. I must have forgotten to dismantle the car's pre-set programming. On autopilot, the Lumina retraced my voyeuristic passes by Karen's house. I wanted to stop several times, but the car wasn't programmed to turn in her driveway and park. Its settings only permitted it to drive by. I had passed by her house at least eight times before I remembered how to manually steer the car. I decided not to beat myself up because of my relapse. I decided to redo this day tomorrow, because I don't have the resolve to start over.

It helped when I blamed Karen. It wasn't all her fault. But then again, if she had not come into my life, our world wouldn't be facing extinction, and I wouldn't know how unpalatable love can taste.

Day eighteen. Almost there.
I had to choose. I had to choose. I had to.

Hubert knew without asking. "I'm down the hall if you want to talk about it," he said during lunch.
"Talk about what?"
"The break-up," he answered.
"How did you know?"
"The gray cloud over your head," he responded.

Twenty-one. I did it. I let her go for twenty-one whole days. That means she should be out of my life.
The truth was I would have loved her anyway. Even if I had known what I know today—that she would abscise us and send our world spiraling out of orbit—I would have still walked that contorted line, fought in vain to hold on to her, and lived again.

Loving her did more than change our life. Her love changed everything. Time was no longer an obdurate reminder of our existence. Minutes. Hours. Days. Weeks. Months. Time didn't exist. So, the tragedy of loving her was not all the conversions she brought to our life. The real heartbreak was that even in the absence of time, there was an ending: a denouement that left us with no tomorrows.

I didn't know who I had become, but I was not the man I was before I met her. On the rare occasion when I was able to summon enough courage to look in the mirror, I barely recognize the anguished reflection staring back. His pain felt like mine. And his tears stung the same. So he and I must be...me.

The sun leered like a Peeping Tom through my window this morning. My T-shirt and my boxers were saturated with the anesthetizing sweat of a hangover brought on by way too many cocktails of darkness and excavated memories. And I was tired...so tired that it hurts to simply be. But my heart—against my will—beat the same. Seventy-three. Seventy-four. Seventy-five beats per minute. Meaning, I was still here. Still here. Still here.

CHAPTER 21

E   very spring Nigel and Caleb took turns ushering the hands
    forward one hour on each of the seven clocks inside their
    house. They did the same during the fall, except they got to
relive the hour they spent waiting to set the clocks' hands back.
Last spring, two hours after midnight on the first Saturday in
April, Nigel expunged an unlived hour of their life. Two weeks
ago, it was Caleb's turn. He began with their official timekeeper,
the grandfather clock in the living room.

It was only an hour. Sixty minutes. Three thousand, six hundred
repossessed seconds. Hardly enough time to choose and live lives
of their own making. But as Caleb circumnavigated the clock's
face aboard the minute hand, erasing the hour between two and
three, he asked Nigel, "If you could do anything you wanted to
during the hour we're losing, what would you do?"

"I don't know," Nigel answered. "I never thought about it."

"Think about it now." Caleb turned and watched as his finger
steered time into its scheduled orbit. "What would you do with
the hour if you were bound only by your imagination?"

Nigel shrugged his shoulders. "I really don't know."

"Come on, Nigel. Do more than breathe."

"I need a minute to think about it." Nigel walked in the den to
change the time on the desk clock. He could have pressed the time
button down, then pushed the hour button once, but he deliberately annulled the hour minute by minute. As he watched the red

digital numbers slowly morph into the next minute and then the next, he considered Caleb's question. Nigel really didn't need to think about his response. He already knew what he would do with the fading hour. He would spend it with Caleb and their mother and father. He would not want their parents to be as they were when they died. He wanted time to have passed for them and given them more years, more stories. They would tell their two sons about their upcoming retirement and reminisce about olden days. They would have no memory of that wintry night fourteen years ago. In this hour, that night never was. He would be the only one present who remembered, because to rid himself of the memory, even in a make-believe moment, could be fatal. He might not be able to return to this life.

"I would spend the hour making love to Karen," Caleb announced to get Nigel's attention.

Nigel put the clock back on the desk, his attention on Caleb. "You would do what?"

"I would spend the hour making love to Karen."

Nigel walked into the living room and sat on the sofa. "You would spend your so-called lost hour making love to my girlfriend?"

"Can the attitude, Nigel! We're speaking hypothetically. What if…"

"Yeah, but your 'what if' is about having sex with my girlfriend. You shouldn't go around talking about having sex with your brother's girlfriend. Not even hypothetically."

"You're right," Caleb said. "My bad. But my advice to you is: if she's your girlfriend, then you need to act like her boyfriend." His apology and advice sounded sincere, but the fire in his eyes betrayed him. If Caleb could do anything he wanted to do with the lost hour, he would do exactly what he said: make love to Karen. He'd fantasized about making love to her, but in this hour it would be real. They'd be alone inside his office where they first consummated their love. He would stand in front of his desk and she'd walk up to him. The fire in their eyes would speak for them as they undressed each other. He'd let his fingers explore her body. He would tease every inch of her body, then kiss her navel and savor her desire. He would make love to her like no man has ever made love to her. Like no other man could.

Caleb tried to hide the mounting bulge in his pants. He fidgeted with a black ceramic ashtray on the stand next to the recliner, then inconspicuously placed the ashtray on his lap. Before Karen came into their lives, he didn't think about women and sex. He accepted the improbability of finding love in his world years ago. But now, all he thought about was making love to her. He'd been staying hard for so long—three, four times a day—that he'd started wearing briefs under his boxers to conceal his restive lusting.

"If I could do anything I wanted to," Nigel said and looked directly at Caleb. "I'd spend the hour here."

Nigel's reverent tone sent chills through Caleb.

"Here?" Caleb asked.

"With you, Mom and Dad," Nigel answered.

"Here with me, Mom and Dad?"

For the first time in fourteen years, Nigel could not stop his heart from declaring, "I really miss Mom and Dad, Caleb. Oh God, I miss them!"

The deluge of tears engulfing him was a measure of Nigel's inconsolable grief and a proverb about the futility of asking, what if.

"So tell me, Caleb. Do I get to live my lost hour?"

"If I had one wish," Caleb extended an olive branch, "you would."

ETERNITY

*Eternity is our lives
before and after
each breath.*

CHAPTER 22 ✧

Karen wanted to be the woman Nigel loved. He was not her first love. She had been in love before. But loving Nigel was unlike loving any man before him. She loved him, the flesh and bone man, and not the beguiling passion of captured love. She wanted to be the woman who caressed Nigel. Possessed and protected him. In return, he would make her whole. She had already accomplished most of her career and personal goals. And she was beautiful. Intelligent. Single and independent. The only thing missing from her life—at least the only thing that mattered now—was someone to share it with. She wanted a man who needed her love and nothing else. A man whose pure touch left her yearning for all of him. A man who wanted to give her his all. And her heart had told Nigel was that man.

Nigel's scars made him even more attractive. His naïveté made him irresistible. And she got high off of his insatiable desire. The marvel in his eyes when he made love to her was euphoric. She was addicted to the virginal sensation of hearing, seeing, and touching him. She could not get enough of him.

Karen didn't stumble blindly into this. She knew Nigel was running from an extant past. That's why she didn't try to get too close too fast. She figured he would open the door when he felt it was safe to let her inside. While she waited for him to let her in, she nurtured her overwhelming need to know him with information acquired by other means. The faculty personnel files provided his home phone number, address, and educational background, but it was a fourteen-year-old front-page article in the *Richmond Times*' online archives that gave her a real glimpse inside his world. The article provided details about a tragic past that he was still living but longing to forget. The article also told her who Caleb was. Even though the information in the news article was public information, she felt she was invading his and Caleb's privacy. But, eventually, she convinced herself that she had a right to know about Nigel's past since she was planning a future with him.

Karen knew who Caleb was when Nigel blurted out his name while she and Nigel were making love in Nigel's office. Blurting out Caleb's name and the confused look on Nigel's face when she thanked him for the tulips made her doubtful about who actually sent them. She tried to ignore the obvious and what it implied, but the truth kept shouting in her ears. *Caleb. Caleb. Caleb sent the tulips.*

Nigel had mostly avoided her since that day. She hadn't seen him in weeks, and he no longer called or returned her calls. She felt she was losing him, but she knew she had to give him space. And he needed time. So today, she committed to giving him space and time.

She missed him already.

A black Lumina with a FAMU faculty decal was in the driveway of 207 Circle Drive. Karen had seen this car before. Her Pathfinder veered off the road, but she regained control and pulled into a parking space by the Myers Park tennis courts. She got out and stared across the street at the black Lumina parked next to Nigel's white Lexus. She remembered seeing the Lumina at the turnpike gas station and parked down the street from her parents' house in Orlando. She recalled seeing the car pass her house; parked across from the gym; and a few vehicles back on the highway. All these sightings were after Barney's funeral but before she actually met Nigel. She started to put the pieces into place, but her heart stopped her. Despite her suspicions that their meeting in the faculty parking lot wasn't pure coincidence, she wasn't ready to know the details surrounding his pursuit of her, at least not while she was pursuing him.

Karen wished she didn't miss Nigel so much. If he didn't occupy every minute of each day, she might not have followed him when she saw him leaving campus. If she had not, then she wouldn't have had to turn a deaf ear to the alarming thoughts reverberating in her head. She decided to ignore the truth that everything about their relationship, beginning with the way they met in the faculty parking lot. Knowing that he stalked her and plotted to gain her affection was damning but not enough to quell her love for him. Instead, she chose to regard all of it as evidence, adjudging it as proof that she was the woman he loved.

Nigel and I shared everything, so why couldn't I remember loving Mom and Dad? Why couldn't I remember being with them? Nigel still loved and missed them, so languishing some-where inside my abysmal memory, was an aggrieved heart.

What happened to Mom and Dad? To me? Those two questions monopolized my thoughts for the past couple of weeks. I could find the answers if I wanted to. They are only a few keystrokes away. However, my fear of the truth had overwhelmed my need to know. So, instead of spending twenty minutes on the Internet today, I flipped through our old photo albums and stared at the pictures on the walls hoping my curiosity could be pacified by the sudden recollection of one of these snared moments.

Nigel hadn't spent any time with Karen. When he's not at work, he's here moping around the house. He'd been trying to keep an eye on me since I started remembering bits and pieces of our former lives. I didn't know how to tell him that he's driving me crazy. Yesterday, I got so fed up with Nigel that I begged him to take a night off his self-imposed exile from life. "Why don't you call Karen so we can get out of this house for a little bit?" I suggested.

Nigel sat on the sofa with his eyes darting back and forth between me and *American Idol*.

"Did you hear me?" I asked.

"You know I usually don't like these type shows," Nigel said, "but this group can really sing."

"I didn't ask you anything about that." I walked over and stood in front of the television. "I was telling you to call Karen and let's get out of this house. We've been stuck in here for the past…"

Nigel cut me off and snapped, "We went to work today and every day this week."

"You're right. But, that's all we do."

"What else is there to do?"

"We can call Karen and go over to her house. We can take her out to dinner or go to a movie, anything other than sitting around in this house every night."

Nigel stood and said, "Karen is no longer part of our life." He walked out of the living room and down the hallway to his bedroom.

When I heard his bedroom door close, I said to myself, "Thanks for telling me we've broken up."

My daily routine changed. I didn't sit by the window all day staring outside at a barbarous and remote world. The world I was discovering inside myself was much more interesting. If I kept following the imbued footprints I left there, I might find me.

I was walking down the hallway toward the bathroom when I glimpsed the framed photo of Nigel being carried off the football field by his high school teammates after he caught a Hail Mary pass for the winning touchdown in the district championship game. Instantly, I was transported back.

I was in the crowded bleachers with Mom and Dad. I heard the crowd celebrating. Mom was yelling, "Nigel! Nigel!" And Dad was leaning over the edge of the bleachers trying to get a good angle to shoot the picture that now hangs on the hallway wall.

Nigel waved to us as the team carried him past the bleachers. "Lil' Daddy! Catch!" Nigel yelled and threw me the winning football. I caught the spiral pass and the crowd cheered even louder. Gradually, their cheers faded with the memory.

I walked inside Nigel's bedroom. As usual, the blinds were closed. A roll of Scotch tape on the nightstand explained Nigel's picket eyebrows this morning. I opened the closet door, hit the light switch and walked inside. The birthday present Nigel couldn't give me because I wasn't speaking to him at the time was on the top shelf. We'd been straight for a couple of months now, so I guessed he's holding it until next year. I knelt and pushed the shoeboxes to the side. What I was looking for was still in the back corner. I picked up the football and wrapped my hands around the memory of that night eighteen years ago.

I was sitting in Dad's recliner tossing the football in the air when Nigel pulled in the driveway. I got up and went to my bedroom. When I heard the front door open and close, I walked into the hallway and yelled, "Lil' Daddy puts it in the air!"

Nigel looked up in time to catch the rambling pass.

"And, Nigel Greene catches it for a touchdown and the district championship!" I exclaimed.

Nigel welcomed this unannounced visit by one of his long-forgotten happy moments with a wide grin and a touchdown ballet. As we danced, I couldn't help noticing a foreboding glare in Nigel's eyes that stayed transfixed on the horizon.

I hadn't forgotten about Karen. Every now and then, I slipped away to be with her. Right now, I had something more pressing on my mind. My search for Lil' Daddy.

I had never wanted to write a blog as much as I wanted to write the one I wrote today. I was excited because this week's blog was the first one based on a real memory. And for that reason, I changed the title of the blog for this week's column. I'd changed the name of the blog before. The last time I changed the blog's name, I wasn't writing about a real memory. I was falling in love with Karen. This time, however, I was hoping it's a permanent change. It probably wouldn't be; I only had a handful of actual memories. But, I was thankful for those few.

The Way I Remember It – by Caleb Greene
"A Cure for Everything"
An aspirin and a hug.
A Coke and a smile.
And, my daddy's belt.
Back in the day, these were my mother's cures for everything that ailed us.

It didn't matter what kind of ailment we were suffering from, one of my mother's cures made it all better. I don't know how she developed these cures, but they all worked. Living with two rambunctious boys, they had to.

There were three types of ailments: physical, emotional, and really bad behavior.

When the ailment was a physical one, an aspirin and a hug was the cure. For minor cuts, scrapes, and bruises, she cleaned the affected area, applied first-aid cream, a Band-Aid, then she dispensed the thing that really made it all better—an aspirin and a hug. For major injuries, she jetted us over to the doctor's office or hospital for professional medical care. Before we left the doctor's office or hospital, we felt better, but we knew the real cure was coming once we got home.

I was around nine when my brother, Nigel, blindsided me during a game of kung-fu and sent me, him, my mother, and father racing to the hospital. We had gone to the movies the night before and seen a Bruce Lee movie. While reenacting some of the scenes from the movie, Nigel decided to improvise and dropkicked me from behind. I landed on a metal can that cut a deep gash in my knee.

Fourteen stitches and four hours later, I hobbled into the house on a pair of crutches and fell out for near-dead on the sofa. "Help me," I moaned as I tried to pull myself up on the sofa.

Nigel raced over to sofa and pulled me up in a sitting position. "Is that good?" he asked in the most piteous of tones.

I groaned and stretched, "Y---e---a---h," into a four-syllable word.

My mother knew exactly what I needed.

"Get me a glass of water," she told Nigel. She rushed to the medicine cabinet and grabbed the bottle of Bayer aspirin, and Nigel ran into the kitchen and filled a glass with water.

Upon their return, my mother could tell I was hurting too bad to hold the glass or the aspirin, so she said, "Try to open your mouth."

Opening my mouth was a Herculean effort. At least, that's what the look on my face hinted. She then placed an aspirin in my mouth and held the glass to my lips while I sipped the water. After swallowing the aspirin, I sighed. That's when she threw her arms around me and hugged me really, really tight and whispered, "Everything's going to be okay now."

And it was. For me at least. But, the look on Nigel's face indicated he was still hurting.

My mother walked out of the living room toward the kitchen. As soon as she was gone, Nigel began stealing glances at me, but he didn't say anything. Finally, he looked directly at me and said, "I'm sorry. I didn't mean to cause you to get cut."

Before I could reply, my mother walked back into the living room.

"Here you are," she said to Nigel and handed him a glass of Coke.

"Caleb knows you're sorry." Then she handed me a glass. "We all know."

Nigel looked up at her and she smiled. He looked at me and I smiled. And the world was okay again for both of us. We were both cured.

As for that other cure of hers—my daddy's belt, I try not to think about it too much. "I don't know what's gotten into you, but don't make me use this belt to beat it out you," she would say and then do.

When it does cross my mind, even now, I can still use an aspirin and a hug.

That really happened, and I had the scar on my knee to prove it.

It was that time of year again. Spring cleaning. Well, to be precise, late-spring cleaning. We usually shake off the previous year's cinders the week before Easter, but this year we waited until the start of dead week, the week before final exams, because there were no classes.

Nigel spent the first day of our pseudo-vacation trimming the hedges, mowing the lawn, and being mimicked by Professor Childers, who pulled out his trimmers and riding mower as soon as he saw Nigel open the garage door.

I tackled the inside. But unlike past years, this year, I was way too excited about dusting, sweeping, and doing laundry. There was something—a scent, a utensil, an ashtray, a feeling—in every occupied space inside 207 Circle Drive that transported me back to the world I inhabited before this one.

I was changing the faded thread on Mom's sewing machine in the den when I remembered Mom sitting at the sewing machine working on a wedding gown. She was putting the finishing touches on a gown for Frankie, who was marrying my cousin, Jerry. I opened the thread drawer and put the black thread back in the drawer and took out a spool of white thread. I threaded the sewing machine and watched Mom inspect the gown as Frankie stared in the mirror and marveled at the beautiful woman wearing her wedding gown.

I walked inside Mom and Dad's bedroom for the first time since last year's spring cleaning and took the curtains down and opened the blinds. As I pulled the patchwork quilt and ivory sheets off the bed, I was back in their bedroom years ago. It was morning. Mother's Day. Mom and Dad were in bed reading the Sunday newspaper when Nigel and I walked into the room carrying breakfast trays. Nigel placed his tray in front of Mom and we yelled, "Happy Mother's Day!" Then I set my tray on the bed in front of Dad and we both said, "That will be five dollars. For me. And for him."

Later that evening, after I remade Mom and Dad's bed and put everything back in place in the room, I walked over to the window to close the blinds and curtains. As the blinds folded in on top of each other, I glanced outside and saw Nigel standing at the edge of Flatley Creek. He was younger; twenty, maybe twenty-one. As Nigel stared at something in the rankled creek, fear chiseled away the look of uncertainty frozen on his face. I closed the blinds, pulled the curtains and tried to forget what I had remembered.

That night I dreamed I was on the other side of these walls. Outside 207 Circle Drive. I should've woken up feeling elated, but in my dream, Nigel and I were beside Flatley Creek. I was wet and lying in the snow. I was dying. Nigel was kneeling beside me, staring frightfully at something in the creek. He was trying to speak, to yell, but he was unable to wrench any sounds from his mouth. Nigel's morbid gaze and my incapacitating pain jabbed me until I woke up, right before I died. I couldn't go back to sleep and I didn't want to.

I was falling inside myself. Plummeting deeper and deeper into an obscure past that, until a few weeks ago, I wasn't sure ever existed. Pray for me.

CHAPTER 24 ✧

God help me.

Caleb didn't tell Nigel what he saw outside their parents' bed-room window, because he wasn't sure what it was he saw. Maybe it was a fume-induced hallucination or an emancipated memory replaying itself. If he had witnessed an actual memory, he deter-mined without question it was a scene from that tragic December night fourteen years ago. Whatever it was, before walking out of the room and closing the door until next spring, he deemed it a mirage, which he figured was more probable considering all the cleansers he'd used that day.

It was almost nine when they sat down to eat dinner—soy chicken and Chinese vegetables—after spending all day Monday sprucing up the house and yard. While they were eating, Nigel looked over at Caleb, who was sitting in their dad's recliner, and asked, "Why did you change the thread?"

Caleb answered, "Mom sewed wedding gowns. I'm assuming that she rarely used black thread. How many wedding gowns call for black stitching?"

"None, if Mom had anything to do with it. The black thread was my doing."

"Why?"

"For no reason," Nigel responded. "One day I walked in the den and changed it."

"Before or after I came home from the hospital?"

"The day before you came home."

Caleb glanced around the living room. "What else did you change?"

"Nothing else. Just the thread."

I'd been telling myself that I'd be ready. That we would be ready. We knew it was coming. So we had to be ready.

The day before Caleb home from the hospital, Nigel stopped by their parents' house. He fumbled with the keys as he unlocked the front door. He turned the doorknob, but several laborious minutes passed before he shoved the door open. Then he stood steadfast in the doorway and waited for the final contractions of his former life to impel him into his new life. He stepped inside and closed the door. He had been inside the house four months earlier installing new storm windows with his uncle and cousin, but it was the first time in two years—since that tragic December evening when he ran inside to call for help—that he was alone in the house.

Nigel had thought about this moment since that December evening. He knew that one day he would have to go back to the house, but it would be after Caleb came out of the coma. Inside, nothing had changed. Their dad's black leather recliner was still by the window. The sofa, the other furniture, and even the what-nots were right where they left them. Their mother's sewing room still shared the den with the family office. Their happy moments were still framed and hanging on the walls and posted on the mantle. Even the air, which should have been stale, was unchanged. Nigel needed to do something to remind him that, although this was still their home, their world was different. Their parents were dead and Caleb had no recollection of their life with them. Nigel knew that if he they were going to stay there, something needed to be different. So, without thinking, he walked into the sewing room, took the white thread off the sewing machine, and replaced it with a spool of black thread. The next day, he and Caleb moved back into the house and began their new life.

These walls, doors, and windows couldn't protect us anymore; the villain was never on the other side. The real threat was hibernating in 207 Circle Drive. Dormant. And waiting. Inside of us. All this time.

Caleb was a sound sleeper until a few days ago when their former life invaded his dreams.

Although it was an unseasonably warm night in May, he was balled up in his blanket trying to ward off the vicious cold of a December evening fourteen years ago. The wind and snow gnawed through time, through the blanket, through Caleb's T-shirt and boxers, to his soul. He knew this was not a dream. Nor was it a mirage. What he saw and felt was the end and beginning of his life.

Nigel's blanket was half on and half off his bed, and he was as sound asleep as he was capable of being since his nightly visits to Flatley Creek resumed. His eyelids were taped opened to keep his dreams from projecting onto them. That was why he didn't feel the scathing cold.

Thursday, December 3rd. The holiday season was in full swing at the Greenes'. Nigel, their oldest son, was a junior at Howard University. He finished his last final exam ten minutes before noon and jumped in his packed car and drove straight to Richmond.

Caleb, the Greenes' sixteen-year-old son, ran barefoot outside in the snow when he saw Nigel's car turn in the driveway a day earlier than expected. Mrs. Greene, carrying Caleb's shoes and coat, rushed outside too. The merry reception in the driveway might have lasted longer than the holidays if Mr. Greene hadn't opened the front door and yelled, "He was home for Thanksgiving, two weeks ago, and you two clowns are acting like you haven't seen him in years. Nigel, come on inside."

Nigel was awakened by the plunging temperature in his bedroom. He double wrapped the flimsy blanket around him and tried to silence his chattering teeth by covering his face with a pillow.

Caleb shuddered as his frostbitten lips were compelled to give voice to a liberated memory. "Mom said she was going to Publix because she wanted to cook Nigel's favorite dinner, which was pork chops and macaroni and cheese. I flashed my two-day-old driver's license in Nigel's face and told Mom I would go to the store. She said the weather was too bad for me to drive, but Dad—to keep Mom from having to go out—agreed to go with me. I grabbed the keys off the counter and ran out the door. I was waiting in the car when Dad walked out the house with my coat. Nigel and Mom stood in the doorway smiling as I backed out of the driveway."

I pray we're ready.

Stilman Road, a narrow two-lane artery that connected the Hinesville subdivision to the Interstate leading into Richmond, crosses Flatley Creek twice. After nearly converging behind the Greenes' house, the road and creek run parallel for about a quarter of a mile. The early afternoon blizzard had repaved Stilman Road with twice as much snow and ice as the tractors plowed off earlier that morning.

"Take your time coming up to this curve, Lil' Daddy."

"Chill out, Dad. I got this," Caleb responded.

"I'm sure you think you do. Damn. It looks like two or three inches of snow fell while we were in the store."

"The forecast predicts five to six inches tonight."

"It's a good thing Nigel left early enough to get here before the storm hits. Okay, Lil' Daddy. You need to really take it easy on this curve. Take your feet off the gas, but..."

"Dad, I told..."

"Don't mash the brakes!"

"Daddddddd!"

Nigel leaped out of bed when he heard Caleb's distressing cry. The blanket was tangled around his legs, causing him to trip and fall. He yelled out, "Caleb!" He ran toward the room. "I'm coming!" It was not the first time he'd shouted these words. "Caleb! I'm coming!" But it was the first time he'd had to relive this scene from that fateful night.

Their mother asked Nigel what grades he expected to get as she cut cookie dough into holiday shapes and placed them on a baking sheet. Nigel gave her the answers she wanted to hear as he leaned on the kitchen counter and stared out the window. From the window, he saw Flatley Creek. He saw Stilman Road on the other side of the frozen creek, and he saw a car's headlights approaching, slicing, swirling. The car, which he intuitively knew was his dad's car, skidded out of control. Uncurbed, it smashed through the embankment of plowed snow and ice on the side of the road. He watched in horror as it harrowed down the hillside before hurtling through the scab of ice covering Flatley Creek. The sleeted water wasted no time encasing and burying the car.

"Caleb! I'm coming!" Nigel screamed. "Dad!"

He ran out the back door, jumped off the steps, and raced across the yard to the edge of Flatley Creek. Before his dive could take flight, a pair of hands grabbed him; his mother's hands.

"No! You stay here," she explicitly commanded. "Do you hear me, Nigel? Stay here! Stay!"

Her dire mandate congealed, hardened, turned to cement around his feet.

Caleb remembered being bandaged by a curdling darkness and silence. Darkness. Silence. Then a flickering light in the distance. A faint noise. A dull vibration that rapidly intensified. He opened his eyes. He was in his dad's car. His dad was unconscious in the seat beside him. He reached over to shake his dad and realized they were not sitting upright. He closed his eyes and hoped he was dreaming. He prayed he was. When he opened his eyes, he saw the mucky bottom of Flatley Creek through the windshield of his coffin.

Caleb heard and felt something pounding on the driver's side window. The pounding continued until the window collapsed from its socket. Flatley Creek poured into the car and filled it until there was only water to breathe. A hand reached inside the car and tugged at his seatbelt. He saw his mother. She was possessed by the unimaginable fear of a mother watching helplessly as her child suffered a horrible death. He would not die; she was not going to let him die. Finally, the seatbelt gave, releasing him. She pulled him out the car and carried him through the frigid water up to the surface. She laid him down at Nigel's embedded feet and instructed her son, "Take care of your brother," before she dived back into Flatley Creek. Back into eternity.

"Caleb!" Nigel yelled as he burst through Caleb's bedroom door into antiquity. Caleb was lying on the floor—beached on the snow-covered shoal of Flatley Creek. His shivering hands reached for Nigel, but Nigel, benumbed by an incensed wind, stood in the doorway staring at two peculiar-looking red water lilies flickering below the surface of the entombing creek.

God help us.

CHAPTER 25 ✧ NIGEL

A new day. In our world, inside 207 Circle Drive, we didn't always wake up to a new day.

We had hidden here in the darkness since time mercifully granted us a furlough from the memory of cemented feet, breathing water, and dying. For Caleb, the tragedy of that day had dawned, and Mom's and Dad's deaths were yet to be mourned. His guilt had yet to be forgiven. Fourteen years had passed since he'd stared at the bottom of the creek like it was his tomb before he was carried to safety, but he remembered it like it had happened the night before.

Before last night, I had forgotten the unbearable pain I'd felt the morning after that night fourteen years ago. Over the years, I'd remembered bits and pieces of the actual accident, but I'd never thought about how I'd felt the morning after. I'd never felt as alone as I did that morning. My parents were dead and my brother was in a coma.

Caleb lay motionless on the floor with his head in my lap for hours. I noticed his eyes gazing at something that I couldn't and probably didn't want to see. As his eyes filled with tears, I felt the hurt he felt. I wanted to help him, but I didn't know what to say or what to do. He was wounded and falling apart, and the only thing I could do was put my arms around him and try my best to hold us together.

The phone rang in the living room. When it stopped ringing, I heard my cell phone ringing in my bedroom. Getting my bearings, I realized that I had missed first period's final exam, and third period's exam was starting in fifty minutes; Dr. Alexander was calling, no doubt to determine my whereabouts. I imagined there was a lot of confusion and cheering outside the auditorium when I didn't show up this morning, but I didn't care right then. My brother needed me and he came first. I had to stay with him. I had to take care of him. I had to.

Karen's staring at us from her picture on Caleb's wall. She's crying but her tears couldn't fall. She realized she couldn't save us.

Caleb sat up, then stood and marched out of his bedroom without saying a word. I hurried out of the room behind him, following him down the hallway. I didn't have to ask where he was going, and I didn't try to stop him. Instead, I closed my eyes and prayed the memory of that night lugged more than unbidden anguish back into our life. Caleb walked straight to the front door. Without hesitating, he unlocked the door, turned the doorknob, yanked the door open, and invited the world inside. I opened my eyes in time to witness the first wave crash into Caleb, surging through his nostrils and fill his lungs. Only this time, Caleb didn't panic. He tried to breathe water, and for a brief second, he did. That's when Caleb's eyes rolled back in their sockets. I managed to catch him before his body fell to the floor. I kicked the door shut as I pulled Caleb over to the sofa.

He wasn't breathing, and he didn't look like he wanted to. "Breathe, Caleb," I yelled. "I said breathe!"

He defied me.

I stared in horror as Caleb tried to die. I didn't think it was possible for a person to will himself to die, but it felt like Caleb insisted on making the impossible, possible. I felt him slipping away. His body went limp and his lips turned bluish-gray. I pounded on his chest to get him to breathe, but he wouldn't. So, I covered his clenched lips and nostrils with my mouth and tried to breathe for him. Caleb still refused to share my will to live. I couldn't stop him from dying, but I could stop him from dying alone.

I ran to the kitchen and grabbed the biggest knife out the counter rack, rushing back into the living room. Caleb was almost gone. I dropped to my knees in front of him and pressed the knife's blade against my neck.

"If you go, I go!"

The knife pierced my skin and blood trickled down my neck.

"Caleb, if you go, I go!"

Caleb gasped, exhaled his will to die, and began breathing. In a voice I didn't recognize, he asked, "Why wouldn't you just let me die?"

I dropped the knife and stared into Caleb's tear-filled eyes. "You're my brother and I need you here. I can't do this without you, Caleb. I wouldn't know how to."

God, please have mercy on my brother.

CHAPTER 26 ✦ CALEB

I killed Mom and Dad.

My brother, Nigel, had been here with me. Here. With me. All this time. Even though he knew what I had done.

When I looked up, I saw dawn encroaching like marching ants through the gaps in the closed window blinds. I saw sunlight. So I knew it must be morning. The morning after I died. But it was still dark and cold here on the floor; a reminder of the dark and cold on the bottom of Flatley Creek where my untenanted coffin rested.

I'd lived like a dead man inside 207 Circle Drive for most of this life. But no more. After dying on the bottom of Flatley Creek. After breathing water. After surfacing, was this life. This world. And my fear. Now that my fear isn't a ghost in the dark, now that I know its origin, I am no longer afraid. No longer willing to live in a pre-empted grave.

I'd walked from my bedroom to the living room countless times, but today it felt like a marathon course. I didn't care how long it took, I was determined to make it to the front door. Nigel was going the distance with me. I felt him behind me. He figured out my destination and he was not trying to stop me, which convinced me that he believed as strongly as I did that I could open the front door and step outside into a habitable world. Flatley Creek filled my lungs as soon as I turned the doorknob, but today, I was not afraid of drowning, or of dying. I'd died before.

Fear was the only thing I was scared of now. Fear. I couldn't live with it anymore. I couldn't and I wouldn't. I'd rather die again.

I tried to die, but Nigel wouldn't let me. He didn't want me to die, so he tried to breathe for me. He tried to share his life again. But it wasn't enough to resurrect my will to live.

My brother wouldn't let me die alone. He's trying to die with me. Trying to share my grave.

I heard Nigel yelling, "If you go, I go!"

I couldn't let Nigel die with me. I couldn't take what's left of his life from him.

I felt the moment my life returned.

"Why wouldn't you let me die?"

"You're my brother and I need you here," Nigel tearfully avowed. "I can't do this without you, Caleb. I wouldn't know how to."

My begrudging tears refused to take sides as I gazed past Nigel at a familiar-looking man hanging from a bed sheet tied to a beam in the ceiling.

This was what I now understood. Remembering did not always erase our fears. Memories merely explained the reasons for our consternation.

The doorbell rang, and Nigel and I both looked up and stared at the door. The doorbell rang again. Nigel stood and, glancing over his shoulder at me, walked toward the door. I pulled myself up off the sofa and retreated to my bedroom. I heard the front door open and close. I heard a man's voice. I opened my bedroom door so I could listen in.

"I called your house phone and your cell a couple of times, but I didn't get an answer."

I couldn't see the man from the doorway of my bedroom, but I recognized his voice. It was Hubert.

"I'm sorry," Nigel responded. "I've been dealing with some personal problems today. I know I should have called, but..."

"Don't worry about it. I have you covered," Hubert cut him off. "I rescheduled your exams for tomorrow since my schedule is open. I stopped by to pick up the exam, and to make sure you and Caleb were okay."

"We will be," Nigel said as he walked into the den. "Let me get the exams."

"I spoke to Karen last week," Hubert told Nigel.

I tiptoed into the hallway and backed into a shadowed corner. I saw Hubert standing near the door. I'd seen him during his class lectures on TV, but he looked different in person. Taller. More self-assured. And a decade younger than his forty-nine years. An aura of fulfillment resonated from within him. Clearly, he was a man who loved his life.

"How is she?" Nigel returned with a small box.

"She's heartbroken. Missing you." Hubert smiled teasingly. "I promised her I wouldn't say anything, but I have to say this. You don't have to avoid her. She knows more than you think she does. And she understands." Hubert grinned and patted Nigel on the shoulder. "She loves you even more now that she knows you spent a few weeks covertly pursuing her before you finally stepped to her."

You could've scraped the embarrassment off of Nigel's face.

"Don't go getting uptight," Hubert advised. "You have nothing to worry about. She loves you, Nigel."

Nigel gave Hubert the box and said, "Thanks. I owe you."

"Then pay me back by calling her. Like I told you before, she's a keeper. Trust me on this." Hubert smiled encouragingly. "I'll call before I bring the exams back tomorrow afternoon."

"I assumed you were going to grade them, too."

"When did hell freeze over?"

Nigel grinned and followed Hubert to the door.

"I told Karen you'd be in touch with her soon," Hubert said.

I slipped back into my bedroom and closed the door. I didn't have to hear the front door open and close to know that Nigel and I were alone again…alone in our amputated world.

We're never unchained.

CHAPTER 27

Take care of your brother. Those were their mother's last words, and Nigel did as he was instructed. He took care of Caleb. Shared his life. Sacrificed dreams. Threw away ambition. And love. All unselfishly.

After learning the truth about that December night fourteen years ago, Caleb felt it was his turn to take care of Nigel because too much of Nigel's life had been lived behind briar-covered walls, too much of his life still unlived. Caleb saw the life he wanted for Nigel when Hubert stopped by the house. Hubert was cloaked in happiness, and Caleb wanted to see Nigel adorned in similar attire. So, he set about tailoring a new life for his brother.

Caleb knew from having shared it that there were two things missing from Nigel's life. The main thing missing from Nigel's life was the freedom to live his life unburdened by the past. The revelations of that December night fourteen years ago had already taken care of that. When Caleb learned the truth about that night, Nigel was released from the burden of secrecy. The only other thing missing from Nigel's life was someone to share it with. Caleb came up with a plan to change that.

That night, when he figured the odds were as close to even as they would get that Nigel was asleep, Caleb tiptoed out of his bedroom, down the hallway, into the living room. He took the phone off of the stand and walked over to the black recliner by the front window. His eyes were drawn to the closed curtains. He parted the curtains with his index finger, and then, with some hesitance, he leaned forward and peered outside at the muddy bottom of Flatley Creek. He was even more convinced that what he was about to do was the only way to save his brother. He picked up the receiver and dialed her number. Since it was a few minutes past midnight, he figured she was sleep. And she was until the phone beside her bed rang.

"Hello," she answered.

"Karen," his voice wobbled. "This is Caleb. Nigel's brother."

He could hear Karen the alertness in her voice when she asked, "Is everything okay, Caleb?"

"It is now," he said. "I'm sorry about waking you."

"Don't be," she responded. "I'm glad you called."

After Caleb and Karen had finished talking, Caleb lay in bed and scoured away the memories of making love to her. He said goodbye to the woman of his dreams and hello to his friend and their savior.

Karen drove past their house three times before her nerves and the morning traffic settled enough to let her turn into the driveway. As she pulled in the driveway behind the black Lumina, she glimpsed a man standing at the front window, staring out through the partially opened curtains. It wasn't Nigel. She was relieved.

A few seconds before the doorbell rang, Nigel heard Caleb run down the hallway and then he heard Caleb's bedroom door close. He debated whether he should get up and see who was at the front door or pull the blanket back over his head and pretend he didn't hear the doorbell. The doorbell rang again, and again, ending Nigel's deliberation. He climbed out of bed and tottered toward the living room. Nigel didn't bother to look through the peephole before he opened the door. He wished he had.

"Good morning." She greeted him with a timid smile. "Caleb invited me over for breakfast. May I come inside?"

"Of course," he answered. "Come in."

Neither Nigel nor Karen expected what happened next. But as soon as Karen stepped past Nigel and inside the doorway into their world, her repressed feelings spilled over. "I love you, Nigel," she cried and flung her arms around him. "I love you."

Nigel tried to speak, to tell her how he felt, but he couldn't.

So she spoke for him. "I know," Karen professed. "I know that you love me. And that's why I'm here."

The elation in his eyes validated her.

She kissed him, softly at first.

He pulled her closer. Close enough to feel her heart beating. He embraced her love, silently thanking God for her.

Caleb smiled as he stood in the living room staring at Nigel and Karen. The door was wide open, but the asphyxiating world outside 207 Circle Drive could not flow past the dams in the doorway. Love. Happiness. Hope. Tomorrow. All dams.

Welcome to our life.

EPILOGUE ✧

After every ending there was a beginning, and this was how our next life would begin.

Fleeing yesterday. Surviving today. Chancing tomorrow. That was how we once lived. Constricted by time and enslaved by memories. But no more. We vowed to change the way we inhabited our stay here. We resolved to seek freedom from our lives. To venture without reason. Pursue possibility. Cater to love. And to not merely exist. No longer would we haul the burdensome heft of our yesterdays into today. This time we would live free.

Truth was all we're carrying into our new lives. Truth; it was an inescapable cage. And how well we accepted this reality determined the inviolable boundaries of our world.

This was the truth…the only truth that mattered.

My brother was beside me when our life ended.
He was with me when this new life began.
He is with me now.
And I will be with him always.
Always.

ACKNOWLEDGMENTS ✧

I'm forever grateful to…
My Heavenly Father
For Life, Love, Blessings, and Dreams.
&
My Mother, Delores
My Grandmothers, Doris and Thelma
For being my unfailing rocks.
&
My Father, Tyrone
My Grandfathers, Willie "Bean" and Lester
For being my steadfast roots.
&
Mrs. Muriel Mixon
(my third-grade teacher)
For opening the door to the world of books with Amelia Earhart's story.
&
You
(one of my Blessings)
For loving me during the hours.

ABOUT THE AUTHOR ✧

Anthony Lamarr is a native of North Florida, where he still resides. He is a graduate of the University of Florida College of Journalism and Communications. A novelist, screenwriter, and playwright, Lamarr is also author of the novel, *The Pages We Forget*.